This novel by Grace Peterson has been preceded by a lifetime of writing, beginning with editorials for her high school paper, which she co-edited. During her 55-year career as a professor of psychology, she wrote case history research reports at the Institute of Child Development, University of Minnesota, which resulted in a life-long interest in the welfare of children. She wrote elementary school curricula for the Minnesota Mathematics and Science Center, Institute of Technology, University of Minnesota. She has also authored many research reports on learning, gambling, environmental attitudes, a statistics chapter, book reviews, and opinion pieces, as well as books on learning, child development, and organizational psychology. Along with her husband, Keith, she edited a book on the organization of the Russian Orthodox Church. She has also been acknowledged for her assistance and editing of several books. With her husband, she has raised an international family of six children.

Grace Peterson

MEGHAN AND BETH DISCOVER, IT'S A MEN'S WORLD

AUSTIN MACAULEY PUBLISHERS™

LONDON • CAMBRIDGE • NEW YORK • SHARJAH

Ordering Information
Quantity sales: Special discounts are available on quantity purchases by corporations, associations, and others. For details, contact the publisher at the address below.

Publisher's Cataloging-in-Publication data
Peterson, Grace
Meghan and Beth Discover, It's a Men's World

ISBN 9798886936698 (Paperback)
ISBN 9798886938654 (ePub e-book)

Library of Congress Control Number: 2024902789

www.austinmacauley.com/us

First Published 2024
Austin Macauley Publishers LLC
40 Wall Street, 33rd Floor, Suite 3302
New York, NY 10005
USA

mail-usa@austinmacauley.com
+1 (646) 5125767

I thank my husband, Keith, for his assistance with this book and for his enduring love.

Chapter 1
Meghan Remembers
Women Talk

Beth reached for her book. People had been whispering about it every now and then over the last few years. There were hushed rumors that the book had something to do with local people or places but never with anything very precise. She had just a few minutes before going to her work at the Graphic Design Shop where she laid out advertising for local businesses. It was finally quiet. Her two children had gone to preschool and her husband had just popped in after morning chores.

"See you later," he said, as he left for work at the local grain elevator. He looked tired. He was trying to run the family farm and work at a paying job as well.

Beth started to read.

Meghan, a twenty-five-year-old Midwestern woman, settled her shapely five-and-a-half feet into her packed black Volkswagen Beatle with red leather seats and a sunroof. Her brown, wavy hair bounced off her shoulders. Meghan was exuberant. *Could life get any better?* she thought. "My new Ph.D. from the University of Nebraska.

A grant for filming a documentary about summer life at a model farm in Iowa. On my way to a professor position at a university in southwestern Minnesota."

As Meghan drove, her eyes surveyed the rich midsummer colors of the blue sky, green corn fields, green puffs of trees like giant pom-poms on the hills, yellowing ripening crops, and pink clover fields. Meghan saw flowers along the roads, yellow daisies, orange lilies, purple flowers on stalks, and even a few pink wild roses. As Meghan passed the miles, her mind began to wander to the last days of her time at the University of Nebraska which had been her home away from home for so many years.

And now she would only spend brief times at her childhood home on a ranch in Nebraska. Still, she was not melancholy about that. She was excited to have new experiences and meet new challenges.

Her mind drifted back to the last get-together of the gang of women friends from the Fine Arts major at the university. They had decided to have wine and cheese for their last get-together. As they were fanning out to distant parts of the country, they wouldn't be likely to see each other much if at all. They got started sounding off on all that had impressed and aggravated them. Just remembering the conversation might qualify for a life-changing experience.

Wow, they didn't hold back, Meghan thought as she re-lived each stunning comment of that entire evening, one by one. She dwelled on their remarks that showed their attitudes toward the male culture within which they had all navigated in their lives. One by one, they joined the conversation with feelings over and over.

'I can't stand any more of these classic males' coming of age books with their descriptions of their first sex experiences. Where are the books by women where they talk about their first sex experiences? I haven't seen them.'

'It's because their first experiences never should have happened!'

'Either a few women were having a lot of sex or these male first experiences were spread out among more women than our culture acknowledges.'

'How could it be any different? Our culture doesn't even know the names of women's body parts in the reproductive system. Take a survey and you'll find out that people, both men and women, will tell you that the reproductive systems are the penis and the vagina. No, they are pathways, the vagina is not a reproductive organ, it is a bag, yes open at both ends, a transmission device.

'I can tell you that women have other important body parts on the outside which are very important for stimulation and satisfaction.'

'There is so much cultural baggage for women to endure. Take religion, for example. It's time for religion to clean up its act when it comes to women.'

'What do you mean?'

'Well, we can start with Adam and Eve. My anthropology teacher calls that story a charter myth, meaning that it is a story of how a group begins. Women's pain at birth is caused by Eve tempting Adam with the apple. She got the apple idea when she had listened to the snake, an event that provided the source for bad reputations for women and snakes alike.'

'Other groups have their own myths as well. A tribe of Native Americans thinks that a sunbeam impregnated the first woman of the tribe.'

'Oh, sure! We need a virgin. Anybody else would already be too dirty! We hear that with the birth of Jesus too.'

'Women aren't dirty! One religion has a prayer given by a leader who thanks god because he was not born a woman. That religion has women taking ritual baths after their periods as if they need to be cleaned up after a natural phenomenon. Women are mammals, for heaven's sake. They have cycles. Who is to say they need cleaning up for any reason or that they should be blamed for any of what goes on with their reproductive system?

'Another religion has a man refusing to shake hands with a woman, even among professors, because of the notion that she is unclean and therefore will contaminate the man.'

'Some native tribes also put women in a special structure during their periods. Pretty scary, we women are.'

'And women get blamed for sex no matter the situation, it seems. A church in my town made a young woman stand up in church and confess her sin which caused her pregnancy. Women are blamed for being temptations was expressed by the head of a religious body when asked why there are no women at their higher ranks.'

'Hey, society has constructed a lot of stigmas regarding sex. It can be too much fun! And blaming women is so handy. They are not supposed to have any sex drive themselves, yet they are the cause of what men do with them.'

'Yeah, blaming women is nothing unusual. I had a boyfriend for a few weeks who decided that he wanted sex one evening. I did not want to engage in sex with him at least at that time. We were graduate students in the same department. I was willing to be hugged and kissed by him but not to have intercourse. He pressured me and begged. "Come on". I finally gave in.

'I was tense and not very responsive, I'm sure. I did not participate but I allowed it. It all seemed very mechanical. Shortly after that, he ended our relationship. He had decided I was not for him for the long term because I had given in to him. Then after breaking the relationship with that as an excuse, he said he had a dream that I was under ice and he skated over the top of the ice.'

'God, what could Freud do with that.'

Meghan had to get her attention back to the road as she had to make sure she didn't miss the exit to a connecting highway. All these remarks had been given her full attention.

'I was so busy with my head in books and papers that I hadn't been thinking how religion can influence and justify people's behavior.'

'I was recently assigned books in Women Studies. These books were written by women. In two books, women who enjoyed sex burned to death by catching on fire while burning trash. In another book, a woman who had succumbed to sex with a charming psychopath died of infection after giving birth to a still born baby and in the fourth book, the main character who enjoyed sex with her friend's husband died of a mysterious disease.

'What is going on? Has the cultural attitude been so burned into us women that this is how we think?'

'You know, we are barely allowed a sex drive in respectable society, so why would it be different in books?'

'You can see how useful women's sex drive can be, though, it gives men excuses for their behavior.'

Beth put the book down. *Whoa!* she thought, her head spinning. She had to get to work. She felt again the stresses of dating, just wanting companionship and some affection but she also got the job of keeping guys' hands off her breasts where they were accustomed to begin their exploration.

"I guess I have been so immersed in child and husband care that I haven't really noticed how other women might see things." *This book isn't what I thought it would be,* Beth thought as she set it aside and hurried to get to work so she wouldn't be late. When she came home after work, she would have liked to continue reading her book but she had to get a meal going as her family would be coming soon.

All the while as Beth was preparing the evening meal, she mulled over religion and women. What really was religion's attitude toward women?

When Beth picked up the book several days later, she didn't know what to expect. The influence of religion on the place of women continued. She didn't go to church often, just enough to please her in-laws who lived in another house on the farm. She continued to read Meghan's friends' remarks.

'There are over one hundred references in the Bible referring to the idea that humans are conceived in sin and that they are born with 'original sin' as well. Again, we are mammals, this is how reproduction works.'

Beth had to put the book down again. This was too much to think about. 'Conceived in sin' bothered her very much. A reference to Psalms 51:5 is explicit: 'I was born in sin and in sin did my mother conceive me.'

"People in church sit in the pews and hear these words. Do they hear? How can humans keep going without children? The Bible directs us to procreate yet if you do so, you have committed a sin. Nature has programmed us to make babies. Nature has put these constrictions on us. This is how babies are produced. Everybody knows that. I don't really think that my beautiful children are products of sin. They are the outcomes of love. Men put this overlay on nature. We have more questions than answers."

Beth opened the book again and read on.

'Oh, but there is a way out, confess to sins that others say you were born with. Then whatever you do (that can be a lot more than sex) can be forgiven. Convenient. Create a need and then show a way to satisfy it.'

'This confession stuff doesn't always work out for people either. My friend thought she would tell the priest her thoughts. The response was "You must be a terrible person". So much for forgiveness for women.'

'Create a need and then show a way to satisfy that need. Classic advertising model. You need forgiveness, tell us about your sins.'

'Good racket. I took a course in developmental psychology. The prof never mentioned that the new infant comes with sin.'

'Well, I've heard the idea that the new baby is self-centered, that is how its sin is shown.'

'What, is it a sin to want to eat? Reminds me of the saying that states that man is a mammal that suckles its young, so eating is necessary for survival. It should be natural and acceptable (except for the man part).'

'In religion class, we learned that church fathers saw anything humans do, which is similar to what animals do, as lower consciousness and thinking in abstractions is higher. Church fathers said that women's role is procreation. One went so far as to say that yes, women could be companions for men, but men would make better companions. So there goes sex, at least heterosexual sex, out the window.

'Charter myths make virgins the only good women, then is it men who bring in the sin part? Oh, that's right, sex we learned is the woman's fault, didn't we? Goes back to the snake, right?'

'Centuries ago, I'd guess that it was common in the Middle East for women to wear headscarves and not speak in sacred places as well as in public. So, it is not surprising that a church father a few hundred years A.D. would prescribe such dress and behavior for women. Centuries later, the prescription continues. Women are restricted from speaking in some churches and not allowed to be spiritual leaders in those religions.

'In some cases, men don't think that they should be under the authority of women even at work. In some countries even today, women are prevented from receiving an education.'

'Male missionaries at my undergrad school came from down south and registered at the school, signing up for a minimal class such as choir while living in a campus house. One morning some college women found this note on their doors. "Are you sorry for what you did last night?".'

'Yes, much harm is allowed under the guise of religion. Mental illness is excused in religion and politics in this country.'

'So, with all these ideas, how can we make women worthy, whole, equal to men? And while we are at it, what about gays, is it time to get those relationships off the sin list? Our religion teacher told us that it is fairly recent in history that same-sex relationships were considered sinful. There can be an economic cost to discrimination against women and gays. A gay teacher was told by a principal that he would be paid the same as women! Where do we even begin?'

'I'll tell you where we can begin. We could look at major religions and find agreement on positive ideas. It seems that in all these religions there are the ideas of hope, love, and service. Concentrating on these would go a long way to make all people worthy and equal. Sex could be removed from the sin list and seen as important in human pleasure and bonding in situations where women are valued.'

Beth had a few minutes before work, so she continued to read. "This book seems to be an attack on religion, but when I think about it, these women's comments show how some women could have negative attitudes toward some religious groups. But I can easily agree with the idea that religion should be about hope, love, and service. A religion based on sin is negative. It's a more positive view to talk about hope, love, and service. Well, let's see what comes next." Beth went on reading.

'You know, we can look at how all this plays out in society, in politics (which seems to be quite affected by religion), for example. People seem to want to believe that religious ideas are OK in politics and even belong in politics. People find it convenient to think that politicians don't really mean what they say about women's roles and treatment.'

'Let's remind ourselves of all the political arguments of recent years and political efforts to control women.'

'Women should not be allowed control over their bodies.'

'Women should not be allowed abortions.'

'Women should not be insured regarding contraception when it is against our values and our religion.'

'Did you hear about the woman on a vacation with her husband in Wisconsin who stood in line at a drug store to buy condoms because she had forgotten her birth control pills? When her turn came in line to buy the condoms, the clerk at this major chain drug store said he wouldn't sell them to her. It was against his values!'

'Yes, remember when all five candidates for a major party stood on stage and stated that they were not only against abortion but they were also against contraception.'

'And then there was the guy who said that if you're being raped, you may as well lay back and enjoy it. There is no enjoyment with rape. It is assault, the same as if someone hits and beats someone. Sometimes there is also a beating. These attitudes toward women go as far as murder after rape. In the rapist's mind, the woman has now been dirtied, had tempted him, and deserved to die. Also, she can't be a witness if she is dead.'

'And the guy who writes on religion who said that it's not rape if a woman doesn't call for help.'

'Well, I have news for him. My friend told me about what happened to her. She accepted a dinner invitation from a fellow graduate student. She was the only one there when she got there as the table was set for two with wine glasses. *OK.* she thought, a nice dinner and conversation. As they were finishing dinner, he came around the table toward her. She reacted to his look and headed for the door.

'She didn't make it. He grabbed her and set her on a high table by the screen door. He seemed very strong and she was immobilized. He pulled down her underwear and started poking into her. During several pokes, she said she did not want to be pregnant. He said she wouldn't and sprayed in a solution. She jumped down and staggered out the door, drove home, removed her clothes, cleaned herself inside and outside, and carried on with her life.

'She decided he must have put a drug in her wine. Although, she had only drunk half a glass, the extreme immobilization seemed to be caused by a drug. That was not sex but assault and there was no screaming for help.'

'Then there was the U.S. Senatorial candidate (note these are all guys) who said if it is a legitimate rape, then the woman can't get pregnant (He lost the election). I wonder where he had learned his biology or sex ed.'

'Oh, we can't forget the judges. Years ago, there was a judge who said that when a woman lies with a man, her body becomes public property.'

'Another judge recently said that a woman invited a man who had helped her in the apartment parking lot up for a beer, she was inviting him to have sex with her, so the judge acquitted the man of rape.'

'The government has a backlog of hundreds of rape kits. That doesn't indicate a very serious effort to charge men with rapes. Police do collect them but that's often as far as it goes. That's not a policy of protecting women. Society and governments are protecting rapists. Consequently, many rapes are not even reported.'

'No, that's more of an effort to service men and protect sperm.'

'Politicians have suggested that women be charged with a crime for getting an abortion. Some have suggested using probes to check for abortions. Lately, there have been threats that women should be followed if they live in a banned state and have an abortion in a safe state. In that case, they should be charged with a crime. That's this country.

'Years ago, guards checked women for blood on pads when they came from East Germany (where abortions were allowed) to West Germany so they could be charged if they had an abortion.'

'Women in some countries are mutilated by removing their parts that contribute to sex drive and pleasure. This procedure results in painful sex and childbirth. I guess that is supposed to make them faithful.'

'That would probably do that if sex were made so painful. Well, at least we don't do that in this country.'

"Small consolation that is," Meghan spoke out loud to herself. She thought, *All this stuff we brought up reeks of male dominance. It is learned young and promoted by customs in society in such a way that people have bought into it, men and women alike. Now that I think of it, I have seen this all my life. My mother told me that when I was two and a half, I was walking up and down on the top of a slanted wall, saying out loud to myself, 'Only (sic) boys do this'.*

"She told me that she said to me, 'You're doing it, so I guess girls can do it too!'. Then when I was in eighth grade, I remember thinking that a neighbor boy was better at math than I was. But I was puzzled about why I thought that because we both got 100s on our math papers."

Then Meghan was reminded of books she didn't like when she was in grade school. "The girl would be involved in some adventure and the book would end up with the statement that she will never do that again. Boys in books had adventures and they were heroic. We can still find books like that.

"For example, one children's book was about a little girl and her older brother. She would try to copy him and fall, so the father said she was good at falling! Others have traditional gender roles such as boys build houses and girls live in them."

Beth set the book aside. She thought, *Meghan is not the only one who has been going over her life and what's been going on around her.* Beth's head felt jumbled. "I haven't paid much attention to current events lately. My thinking has been dominated by meals, children's forms, and housework. Then there are doctor's appointments for the children, phone calls, for arranging appointments for the house and farm, and requests from my in-laws.

"All that besides my graphics' job. Now I am hearing movements to ban abortions and even birth control. Why so much need to control women? I have read and heard stories of unwanted pregnancies in earlier days. Women tried to create their own abortions and sometimes died. They felt forced to marry men with whom they were not compatible. Pregnant teenage girls were sent out of town and often didn't get to finish high school.

"I know men especially argue that these women shouldn't have had sex if they didn't want the consequences. My answer to that is 'Tell that to men'. I know that there have been changes in some of these situations from earlier days, but would we want any of those days back again? I'd say, 'Yes, we are talking about a potential child but the pregnant woman is already a complete human being. We are choosing'. All this attention to women's reproduction makes me nervous. My mother just says, 'It's women's business'."

Beth continued reading.

In her head, Meghan could hear the voices of her friends back at school as she drove along. She continued her mental review of the conversation as she drove along.

'All this stuff we brought up describes the male dominance that girls and women experience. It is learned young and promoted by customs in society in such a way that people have bought into it, men and women alike. I visited a preschool the other day and a three-year-old boy was telling a three-year-old girl she couldn't climb up the ladder of the slide, that girls couldn't go on the slide.

'I went over to the slide and intervened. I said, sternly, "Yes, girls can use the slide!". I told the little girl, "You can go down the slide". She shook her head from side to side and chose not to go down. This is how young male dominance starts. We learn to move over for the boys, and it lasts a lifetime.

'Boys even use aggressive tactics such as grabbing girls' body parts or clothing in high school and have been observed punching women's arms in college. We must even sit tightly while guys spread all over.' Meghan renewed her review of her friends' comments.

'My women's studies prof asked us why we thought women were dominated even in matriarchal societies. No matter how tasks were divided by gender (in all societies), women's tasks were less valued. For example, in some societies, men made baskets, other societies women did. Basket making was more valued if it was done by men, less so if by women. The students were asked why this male dominance seems to show up in every society.

'Finally, a young man spoke up, "Because they are bigger?". Male dominance shows its extreme in rape and spousal abuse where being bigger counts.'

'At the 15th high school reunion after the meal, the entertainment was pornographic movies in a separate room for the guys. Women were not welcome. A few women may have de-segregated the audience but most just sat together and talked. Some out-of-town spouses who had married women from the town were quite shocked and didn't go in either.'

'In grad school, I went to a faculty retirement party. A male prof conducting the program reminisced about their Friday afternoon beer outings where among other things, the male profs there talked about what the female faculty would look like undressed! I know the women profs didn't conduct a reverse discussion.'

'When I came to graduate school, I expected to be treated better in academic institutions than I had been in other places, that is with less male dominance than I had found on dates or at work. Here, I had all those credentials and high goals of what I could do there. A prof gave me a ride home and, on the way, he put his hand on my thigh.

'Here, I had been thinking I had moved out of the "prey" category into a more respectful place for women, only to find that I was still classified as an ordinary female. Touch is an important way that male dominance is expressed.'

'Even if we move out of the prey category, we enter a milieu of derogatory comments such as you think like a woman, unfeminine, and other descriptions. These don't work as well these days, so when men want to dominate women, they denigrate women's credentials, their degrees, their intellectual work, and performance. "Women in graduate school are not as creative as the men".

'This attitude of a well-known psychologist can carry on into the academic workplace. "We can hire a woman if she is qualified" spoke a faculty male on a selection committee.'

'A twenty-one-year-old accomplished violinist and other young women who came to play in a national orchestra were called bimbos by the young men players. At first, the women tried to laugh but they soon found out that it was not funny as the guys competed for the best placements. My women's studies teacher said that respecting credentials is the next big battle after male predators treat professional women as objects for prey.

'Treating women's credentials respectfully could take care of the "Me Too" concerns as men might be less likely to grope women whom they respected for their competence.'

'There is a certain amount of men's world vs. women's world. A man described an ideal experience as time up north in a cabin with boots unlaced, beer, with no shaving, and no showers. In other words, no women and no need to impress them. Many women don't feel a sense of companionship with their husbands whose attention to sports dominates holidays and weekends over family time.

'Some men feel the need to get away from women, so their worlds intersect only in certain ways for certain activities. They then go back to their own world.'

'Though there is tension, the culture has accepted the male version of the world. Why are so many words connected with sex also considered negative or inappropriate nouns and adjectives? Look how the f-word is used, and how words for women's body parts are used as accepted expletives. What really is being expressed here?'

'Men talk and they boast about exploits of their male dominance. My friend told of a guy from work who gave her a ride home after work one day. Before leaving the car, she told him to stop his attempt at sex. He later bragged to his male buddies that he could get a Mack truck in there. Most people probably didn't believe him.'

'That's the best excuse for a small penis I've ever heard!'

'And girls think that they must pick from the guys who pay attention to them, like multiple choice. But not all women follow that principle. I read that Ayn Rand didn't follow that male dominance stuff. She would give a signal and the husband of a friend would follow her to the bedroom for sex. I wonder what the conversation was like between the spouses left behind.'

'I went to a talk by a well-known psychologist who was speaking on a psychological principle named after him. He hadn't discovered the behavior but had given it a name, a way to get fame that while important is not as creative as discovering the principle. Anyway, I'm sitting in a large auditorium, people all around. He is talking about consequences and uses the word, scoring.

'Obviously, he is referring to a man's ability to get sex with the connotation of winning in a dominant way. I felt myself get literally smaller, shrinking, in my chair.'

'A friend's young daughter described how intercourse works. She said, "The woman lays her vagina over the penis". That's a good start to a better story of a pleasurable first sex experience from a woman's point of view. Maybe we can start with that as we look at the description of a positive first sex experience that my friend and I put together.

'Here's a kind of description that we would like to see in books. "He and I had just experienced a very emotionally charged movie about a loving couple who had a baby by the end of the movie. So already with highly charged emotions, we lay down on his bed. We embraced from head to toe, no space between. This was very different from being in a car's front seat being hugged, kissed, and touched. Consciousness of my surroundings left me.

'"I felt my body parts between my legs awakening, swelling and tingling. Suddenly, I was underneath. The penis was touching me, separating my labia, going down over other parts. It found the opening and pushed inside. For a moment, all was still. The penis fit the inside space where I wanted it to be. Then down, up, down, up again and again. Suddenly, it was out and spouting like a geyser.

"'I looked at him in wonder and amazement. I had become a changed being. I became conscious of my surroundings again. I picked up my underwear. I had no idea when they had left me".'

"That's better," Meghan reacted out loud as she remembered this version of a woman's first sexual experience. She thought that this was way superior to being a recipient object of a man's experience. The issue of consent didn't seem to be an issue there. Consent is an issue with new acquaintances and short-term dating.

Men are supposed to ask women if they can go ahead with sex, but research suggests that even if a woman doesn't want to engage in sex, she feels pressured to agree to avoid hurting a man's feelings. What feelings? Self-centeredness, indifference, disrespect? Is such a man really trying to show he values a woman or just 'scoring?' Under those conditions who can feel much sexual satisfaction or worthiness?

Meghan continued passing mile markers on her way to her summer film grant position. She remembered what a friend a few years older had said once in a discussion about having children. 'My body wanted a baby', she had said. Meghan hadn't thought much about it at the time, but now, she said to herself, "A baby, maybe not, but my body wants something." Meghan hadn't paid much attention to guys in the graduate department.

While she worked with some of them, she was too focused on projects to notice them as potential dates or husbands. Every now and then, one of them would become engaged and she'd think, "Really, he was a possible guy? I've been on birth control pills to monitor monthly cycles, which could have been used for birth control, but I never needed them for that!"

Beth had a pop-up memory and stopped reading. She was back in her teens standing in the entry of her family home, kissing her boyfriend good night. He held her tightly and suddenly, it seemed he had a vertical flashlight below his waist pressing against her tummy. Surprised and maybe a little horrified, she asked, "What's that?" Beth couldn't even remember his explanation; she was so shocked.

"I had a father and brother but I had never seen an erect penis. Well, look at the sex education I've had. The biology teacher had cut out the chapter on men's and women's body parts and reproduction. That's what people said, anyway. Later, I found out what a penis can be used for!"

Beth's mind returned to the present and she opened the book and read more on Meghan's trip.

Chapter 2
Meghan Studies Farm Life

Meghan's drift into the past shifted to attention on the road. She needed to find the exit to the small town and the motel where she had reserved a room for the month that she would be filming and writing on the sociology of farm life. She caught sight of the motel sign, turned into the driveway, and parked her car. As she registered, she thought that the clerk looked at her quizzically.

Finally, she couldn't contain herself and asked what Meghan was going to be doing all that time. Meghan said, "I'm going to be studying and filming farm life."

"Will people here get to be in the movies?" The clerk inquired.

Meghan responded, "Probably not many people, just those connected directly with farming."

"Too bad, not much happens around here, so we're looking for some excitement," the clerk answered.

After checking in, Meghan studied her materials. She was expected at a farm about twenty miles away. A graduate agricultural student who was managing the farm that summer was to meet her there. He was part of a program that sent advanced students out to gain practical experience on modern farms.

Meghan called him and made an appointment for the next day. The next day when she arrived, she parked and rang the doorbell. "Whoa," she was shocked. She had imagined an older, more senior individual. This guy was tall with brown wavy hair and broad shoulders and seemed to be about her age. Meghan was glad she had discarded the hair bun when she left campus and now had wavy shoulder-length hair.

"You must be Meghan," he said. "Welcome to the model farm, I'm TJ. Come in for coffee and we can talk about what we will be doing for your project."

After some more chit-chat about weather and general farm topics, Meghan began to describe her film project as a documentary about farm community life, changes, and how people are adapting to those changes. "I would like to interview you and other farm families around here regarding their views on their activities and how they see outside influences on them.

"I want to describe their typical days as well as events they see as opportunities or threats. In general, I will use a rural sociology approach that includes main institutions such as churches and schools. I am hoping to include you in part of the filming."

TJ responded, "I will make introductions for you in the community which should help you get started. Also, there may be some places I could go with you depending on our time schedules. Besides farming operations, my task here is to analyze the economic data on this farm and compare that to other public data."

Meghan replied, "I, myself, grew up on a farm. I decaued farm life was not for me when I raised a pig and a calf. I calculated that I got about five cents an hour after paying for feed. Then I was slight of stature and my calf got too big and pushed me into the gutter. So, I went to college for a different career. However, I am also interested in the economics of farm life as well as government policies for farmers.

"There seems to be a trend toward larger and larger farms. I would like to hear the reactions to that trend from farmers themselves. I'm also interested in any adjustments they are making to climate change."

"First, today I will show you around this farm which is primarily a hog, corn, and grain farm. Most dairy farms closed when milk policies changed with a new administration, so farmers adjusted by changing which crops and animals they raised," TJ offered.

They agreed that they would meet back together later in the day to look around the farm. Meghan worked with her camera equipment and went about the farmstead looking for good photo shoots. She decided to wait until filming for better lighting. Later, with the sun in a better spot, she found TJ and had him appear in the first filming of the project. They got on an ATV and he pointed out the corn fields on the flatter land.

When the terrain began to get hillier, the grain fields emerged. He showed her a small area where the terrain plateaued. There was no crop planted there. TJ called the field a prairie. It had never been plowed so it was a pristine prairie with long green grasses, and pink, yellow, red, and purple wildflowers, and even wild strawberries. Meghan thought she would like to visit the wild strawberry patch and perhaps pick some of the berries.

She liked strawberries, especially wild ones. After the tour, she agreed to come back to photograph farm fields and the hog operation. Meghan told TJ that she would be back in two days to discuss what's next after she interviews the town newspaper editor and other folks at farm-connected stores.

Meghan went back to the motel to map out her next two days. She would like to also go to cafes where older and retired farmers collect but she would wait for TJ to accompany her. That would make it possible to spend time listening as well as asking some questions. She made an appointment at the newspaper office. Her thoughts occasionally drifted to TJ.

The next day, Meghan, who had previously told the editor of her plans, went to his office at the local paper, *The Ledger*. The editor greeted her warmly. "Welcome to our town, Meghan. I'm happy to take this time with you but some comments will be for the record and some off the record. I know from what you have said that you are interested in looking at the situation in the farming community as well as any changes occurring here.

"I am very concerned about our town and the farmers surrounding it. The federal farm policy changed for dairy farmers and many couldn't shift from dairy to corn and grain to stay in business. They could have an efficient dairy farm even if it was small but many of them did not have sufficient land to switch and had to go out of business. That came close to shutting down the town.

"The federal farm policy has been to make farms 'efficient' which meant larger farms. The small farmers often must sell their land when they can't make enough money to live on. Sometimes they keep the homestead and one or both of the couple have to get jobs in town. It is like being on a conveyor belt with the inevitable end, small farms disappearing."

"Thank you very much for that summary. How about on the record now," Meghan said. "Do you see any opportunities for farmers to stay on the farm?"

The editor answered, "The farmers often have to drive to work in a larger city now. They sell or rent the land and stay on the farmstead, but some are moving away into this town or larger towns. Our town is becoming a bedroom community now instead of the economic center of a farming community. Churches close and schools close and consolidate. We lose community centers.

"So, there can be many economic, social, and political adjustments. Some folks have become very creative with crops which bring town folk to them, such as becoming a pumpkin farm with fall activities. Some have converted farm buildings to rent for country weddings and so on. Some have contracted with stores and restaurants to raise food directly for those places. But there are only so many who can get customers to replace farm crops."

"I'll certainly look for such creativity as I visit local farms. I will be asking people what they are predicting and what their ideas are for responding. Thank you for your time," Meghan said as she left.

The editor followed up with some advice for places to visit. "Be sure to go to the hardware store, the feed store, and the grocery store. I know the owners will have some comments."

Meghan spent the rest of the day visiting various establishments in the small town. Most of their comments centered around concerns for the future and how they would adjust to the decline they feared. The owner of the feed store remarked, "My income is down as the number of farms goes down. The young and smart people are leaving. We are having a brain drain from the county which leaves us with fewer human resources. They say there is no place for them."

Meghan finished her day and returned to the motel feeling low.

Beth finished reading about farm policy and knew exactly what they were talking about. These were the adjustments she and her husband had made to stay on his parents' farm. By doing that, they were able to make enough money for themselves and their parents, but their jobs depended on the small nearby town. "Would we have to drive further in the future to get to other jobs? And how will his parents manage?" They had already seen so much change in the economy. This change didn't only affect the farm economy, change also affected their personal lives.

Beth looked down at her outfit of slacks, t-shirt, and sweater that she was wearing for work. That alone was a change for them. "Why, my mother and mother-in-law would get frostbite on their legs before putting on slacks for church. They didn't even cut their hair because there was something in the Bible about women not cutting their hair. The Bible says that women shouldn't wear men's clothes, so when my husband's older brother needed some new jeans, his dad brought a pair home from the store.

"His brother responded with horror, 'Those are girl's jeans. Look at the zipper on the side!'. His mother watched the scene and decided there were special slacks for women, so then women wearing slacks wouldn't be wearing men's clothes. That still did not change his mother's outfits, however, no matter if it was forty below. If they have trouble adapting to clothing styles, how can they adjust to the loss of farms and small towns?"

Beth had to get to work now, the book would have to wait for another day.

"This book reminds me of many memories," Beth said to herself as she picked up the book again. Her husband had taken the children outside to play. She began reading more about the farmers' comments.

Meghan had supper at a local restaurant and looked at her notes as she ate her meal. A few customers glanced at her. The owner came over and asked if he could join her. He asked, "I see you seem to be still at work. You're new here or just passing through?"

Meghan answered as generally as possible, "I'm studying farming communities under the auspice of the university. Do farmers collect here mornings for coffee at any regular time of the week? Maybe I could listen to their concerns?"

"Oh, there is a group of older folks who come in every morning at about 10. I'm sure they'd be more than happy to tell you their thoughts."

"I'll be in within the next days, I'm sure. Thanks for the information."

Back at the motel, Meghan typed up the notes she had taken during the day and added her reactions. *There's an undercurrent of anxiety in the countryside. They worry about government policies, the market, taxes, satisfying regulations, their own finances, and of course, weather,* she wrote.

The next morning, Meghan checked in at the farm. TJ was sitting at the kitchen table with a cup of coffee. He poured a cup for her and sat down by her around the corner of the table. TJ seemed in a low mood.

"Yesterday, there was a farm auction down the road," he said. "I thought I would see for myself the situation that farmers are talking about. The farm owner of the land being auctioned was sitting on a chair at the front of the gathering crowd. I introduced myself and he began to tell his story. He had come up short of cash even after crops were sold. He needed $20,000 to keep going.

"He went to a government farm official in the city fifty miles away to try to get a farm loan for that amount. The government representative told him, 'We can't give you $20,000 but we can give you $100,000 for a hog barn'.

"He told him, 'I don't need a hog barn and I don't see how I can make enough no matter what I do to pay back such a big loan'.

"The response was, 'Take it or leave it'. He said, 'OK', and hoped for a miracle. 'The miracle didn't come and here we are', he said with tears in his eyes. 'My wife has a job in town, and we can stay in the house for now. Most likely my richer neighbors will buy the land'."

Suddenly, a group of people showed up along with a senator. They moved to the front. When the auctioneer stood up to announce the beginning of the sale, the group immediately surrounded the podium chanting, 'No sale today'. They kept it up for an hour. The auctioneer canceled the sale at least for that day.

"I don't know what is happening in the countryside," TJ lamented. "My professor at the U said that farmers had to feed the world and to do that they had to be efficient. He didn't say that some farmers had to be driven out to do it."

Meghan sympathetically put her hand over TJ's hand. He was obviously puzzled and hurt. "Something is going on with a whole way of life. How will I be affected? How can I keep up with the changes? I've understood that farms would have to be run as efficient businesses. I have studied spreadsheets and I know how to keep track of accounts. But what other changes are coming?"

Obviously, the auction and the protest to stop the sale had been very upsetting to TJ. After asking his permission, Meghan decided to take notes on what TJ was telling her. They went out to stroll around the farmstead. Meghan watched TJ feed the hogs and check on their health. They discussed the schedule for meetings in town when local farmers would be in the restaurant. They agreed that they could do it tomorrow.

Meghan and TJ met at the local café the next morning before the local farmers gathered for their morning coffee. This was a typical small-town café with the specials on the blackboard, a counter with stools, and the cash register at the end by the door. The ceiling had large, white metal tiles with designs on them. There were red and white checkered curtains on the windows and red and white oil cloths on the tables, most small and one large table.

Meghan and TJ sat down on the stools by the counter and Meghan set her camera down. They planned to ask to join the others at the table where the farmers would gather. They remembered from college that you don't sit in someone else's customary spot, not when you want to converse with them. They ordered coffee and rolls and waited on the stools for the gathering of local folks.

Locals, including farmers, began to stroll in and take their own spots around the large table. Most seemed to be in their sixties. Meghan and TJ asked if they could pull up chairs and join them. They explained that they had come from the university where there are people who want to get a better understanding of the farmers' current situations.

Several of the men gave a friendly gesture to invite them to join in the conversation. They seemed happy to hear that anyone was interested in them. Several men began discussing the current weather and forecasts. "Got a good shower last night. Good for the corn and beans." The conversation moved around the table.

"Grain could use it too. Knocked down a little grain, but it will come back. We sure need a better sale price than we had last year. We got some government help with loans, but it was barely enough to keep going. If we don't get a better crop this year, I'll have to decide if it's time to retire."

"Joe down the road is selling out his machinery this year and renting his land. Farmers around here think they must get bigger and bigger to stay in business. Sometimes I think that getting bigger and bigger just makes your losses bigger!"

TJ asked what they see as problems coming up. One fellow responded, "We can't get along without government programs. We'd like to but we can't control our costs and sale prices enough to get along without them. Then we can't just choose what crops and how much we want to raise. We have to keep track of what is getting passed in Congress and just take what we get. We had a congressman who did the best he could in a country where only about one percent is in agriculture."

An older man who had been sitting quietly spoke up. "Funny thing about this country. The only time we can make money is when there's a war."

"Yah, we don't control very much ourselves."

"We must get bigger to be more efficient. I've got three thousand acres now. It still doesn't seem enough."

TJ asked, "But how did you get all that land?"

"I bought the neighboring farms when they weren't efficient enough."

All was quiet.

TJ sensed some tension. He broke the silence and asked, "What kind of plans are you making for the future?"

A man who had been listening to this conversation began speaking slowly. "There are so many factors we don't seem to be able to control, it makes it hard to plan. There's the weather for a start, the farm programs which seem to change regularly, not to speak of the fact that some people in Congress think that it's a 'moral hazard', meaning you can't have people dependent on the government by getting any financial support.

"Then there is the export policy which changes with administrations. Large corporations seem to be in charge of agricultural policy these days. I read that people in New York who are not even farmers, but who apparently own land, receive many of the subsidy payments. We also have our health expenses. We are getting older and the hospitals and clinics are moving farther away from us."

"We want to keep the lifestyle of farming, not just be managers for large owners. We want to keep farms in our families, but it is getting harder to do that. We need some sense of where we are going."

"Yes, remember the days when the farms were smaller. We knew our neighbors and the farm extension agent would visit us, telling us what was new?"

"Yah, those were the good old days, that's for sure."

Meghan summarized the discussion with, "Thank you all for your frank comments describing where we are now in the rural region. We understand the real problems farmers have now. We hope our projects can alert people who make decisions that affect you all." She asked, "Would you all please sign your names on a sheet giving me an OK to take a photo of all you good-looking guys?"

Beth put down the book. "This is upsetting. It is too close to home. Farming probably never was easy." She remembered her old neighbor who told of his plight during the Great Depression. "He took a load of corn to the elevator to be shelled and sold. The elevator manager told him the bottom had dropped out of the price of corn. The manager could only pay him 2 cents a bushel but he would still have to charge the traditional 3 cents a bushel to shell it.

"The neighbor's grandson used a variation of that price-cost plight in his act as an amateur juggler. When he performed at a Farm Bureau meeting, he explained how he had learned to juggle using eggs. It cost his family 10 cents a dozen to produce the eggs and when they sold the eggs, they could only get 5 cents for them. Thus, every time he broke a dozen eggs, he saved his family a nickel!"

Beth continued with her thoughts. *When the relatives came to America, they weren't necessarily farmers but they could get land and they could learn farming without knowing much English. Her mother-in-law told a family story that her dad had told her. He said, 'One day, my dad brought home a single plow for a horse to pull. He proudly presented it. I thought, what am I supposed to do with that dinky thing?'*

His father surely saw that thought on my dad's face. At that moment, the father became the past, and the son, the future. My dad later got a two-bottom plow for horses and still later a tractor and plow. My mother-in-law remembers following the plow that turned up turtle eggs in the field next to the lake and taking them home to try to hatch them. Now farmers try to farm with minimal or no tillage, so plowing, too, has passed on.

"Farmers are contracting with a whole new business that would electronically measure and map the areas of soil compaction in their fields. The company would then recommend the least tillage necessary to reduce the soil compaction." Beth thought, *the computer has become part of my husband's machinery, hard to fathom.*

Beth went on to think of her mother-in-law's grandfather who had come from Sweden, married a Swedish woman, and bought a farm during a war when prices were high. He lost it in the next decennial recession (depression, panic, or whatever you want to call it, it's all the same) that the U.S. seems to need every ten years or so.

He still had to repay the loan. He and his growing family moved from farm to farm for the rest of their days.

When they had accumulated things, their house with an organ and five gold pieces burned down. Her father, the youngest child, looked through the ashes for days but never found the gold pieces. Her grandfather had never been a farmer but what else could he do in a new country where land was all around? He wanted to go back to Sweden but his wife reminded him there was nothing for them there.

Her grandfather and his family brought over their parents, grandparents, and an aunt. In the old country, they were responsible for their elders. But their hopes now resided in their offspring. Her grandfather died of a bleeding ulcer.

Beth came back to the book several days later. There had been much to think about farming as a career. Her thoughts about her husband's family history and the stresses today were almost overwhelming. She had been keeping this book to herself rather than discussing it with her husband and it seemed best to keep it that way. Now Beth did want to get back to see what was happening with Meghan and TJ. She read on.

Meghan rode back to the farm with TJ. He pointed out landmarks that might interest her. When they got to her car, she reached for his extended hand and gently squeezed it. Meghan returned to her motel after they had agreed to a noon appointment to photograph the farm fields. She found a bouquet of roses in her room with a card from TJ. Meghan was touched by that gesture.

She called him to thank him and they agreed they looked forward to the next day. Meghan got some take-out food and typed up notes on the restaurant conversation and her own observations of the conversation.

The next day, Meghan arrived at noon. She joined TJ for sandwiches at the table. They summarized their reactions to yesterday's events with a sigh. Meghan said, "They fear hard times coming. We hope we can contribute by sharing their fears with a wider audience and that there will be a response to the issues."

"Today, let's enjoy this great weather and head for the fields," said Meghan. They got on the ATV. She sat behind him and put her arms around his waist. They started their tour with the grain fields. The wheat field was turning gold and the background of windbreak trees made a beautiful contrast where Meghan had to stop to appreciate and photograph. She went into the woods to get another shot.

Soybean fields and corn were next. The rows of corn plants with their long-tapered leaves showed interesting angles with beautiful close-ups. The soybean fields were turning a beautiful shade of mauve in the sunlight. Meghan said to herself, "I understand the love and attachment farm families have to the land."

Next, they headed for the prairie Meghan had seen on the first tour. The original prairie land was a gentle picture of waving grasses, colorful flowers, and wild strawberries. They stepped off the ATV and took in the scene. "Here's some strawberries," Meghan called. They picked some and ate them as they picked. Meghan picked up her camera and started recording the beauty all around.

She stopped photographing and looked into TJ's eyes. She realized that he had been watching every move of her body as she bent and stretched to get just the right photographic point of view.

As Meghan and TJ looked into each other's eyes, both pairs of eyes said, 'Yes'. She set her camera down and they both sat down beside it. She felt his arms around her and sensed her lying back. They faced each other with an all-body hug out there among the wild strawberries. She felt hands touching her body and her lips pressed on his. She heard TJ say, "You are so beautiful." She pressed her body to his.

She sensed a swelling in each of their lower parts. Meghan unzipped her jeans and got help removing them and laid on top of them for a grass covering. She felt hands along her body, on her breasts under her shirt and down her sides, and down to her thighs, hands that moved to parts that were tingling with pleasure. Her legs were ready to spread as she felt the penis enter between the labia, down past the vulva, and slide inside of her.

Meghan's body had what she wanted now. Thrusts of the penis over and over were both soothing and exciting. Feeling more and more excited, Meghan felt an extra thrust. The excitement was at its most possible intensity. Nothing existed except the intensity between her legs. Then the intense feelings all subsided as she felt his body rest on hers. She felt a warm glow within her abdomen. She was holding him tightly.

They rolled sideways still attached as they rolled and then lay side by side in peaceful calm. Meghan looked at TJ with surprise and wonder and said to herself, "This adds a whole new dimension to our university projects."

They got presentable and Meghan felt a hug. She felt her hand slide into TJ's as they strode to the ATV. Back at the farm, she felt a kiss on her lips as she got into her car. TJ looked at her with a soft look on his face and said, "Thanks for a wonderful day."

"Yes, it was a wonderful day, let's meet again sometime," Meghan smiled. Through the car window, they discussed where she should go to start the next day's interviewing of farmers. He suggested she interview two women down the road who were running a small farm where they raised goats. She headed back to town and the motel for the evening. Her notes didn't record everything from that day.

Meghan headed out to the goat farm the next day. TJ had done some introductory communication with neighbors about Meghan's project. This helped to reduce suspicion and promote cooperation and prepare the way for Meghan. She arrived at the farm where goats were immediately obvious as several of them came to the fenced area to inspect the newcomer. Martha came out of the house and welcomed her. Meghan explained her mission and offered to come at another time if this time was not convenient.

"No, this is a good time," said Martha. Meghan had some prepared questions but was ready to follow up with any leads that seemed too good to drop.

Meghan asked Martha to briefly describe her Alpine goat operation. Later, she would ask about what opportunities Martha saw in staying in the country on a small operation and what threats to her way of life that she saw. Martha answered, "We, that is, my daughter and I have twenty-five Alpine goats. We have enough space and grass for the goats. Goats are a possible option when a person has small acreage.

"We had a small farm and we had to sell off the land when my husband became ill. Before he died, we planned together what would be a viable option for living in the country. We were able to keep the farmstead with a few acres. So, we are glad for that."

"What do you do with the goats to make money?" Meghan asked.

Martha answered, "Right now, we sell goat milk at a local store and to neighbors. But we are working on establishing a cheese-making facility. My daughter is taking a class on cheese-making from goat milk and we intend to start soon. We are working on a contract with a grocery store in town and hope to develop a mail-order business. By joining in with a local business that sells sausages, we hope to advertise in their catalog as well."

"It sounds as if you have any questions and answers on your opportunities well thought out. Do you see any threats to your plans?"

"No, our biggest task will be to build up a brand. We will advertise and give small samples at the grocery store. Of course, we will be at risk for problems that come along in the general economy, but we hope to weather even that with local connections."

Meghan suggested that she would like to film Martha, the goats, and the farm. Martha walked around with Meghan and her camera. They chatted as they walked. Meghan asked Martha if she knew the people a mile down the road. When Martha said she did, Meghan asked her if she would phone them on her behalf to indicate that Meghan was planning to stop there the next day. Martha agreed.

The farm down the road that Meghan planned to visit was very large, several thousand acres. When Meghan got there the next day, the man who had collected all that acreage was there to meet her. He immediately spoke loudly, "I hear you want to talk to farmers in the area. My farm is an excellent example of an efficient farm now and in the future. Here, we raise only corn and grains, no animals. It's more efficient to raise animals on the factory farms.

"They often do that on contract so they can keep their land. People like that could sell to me. That's how I have collected three thousand acres, by buying out farmers who weren't efficient. Been doing very well at it, very well at it too, I can tell you. Come, I'll show you around," he gestured proudly. Meghan and he walked around a sample of that farm and she filmed some of the fields so large that you couldn't see the end of them.

Next, she went on to a farm called Twin Forks Dairy Farm. She didn't see any dairy cattle anywhere as she drove up to the farmstead. The owner was sitting in the yard. Meghan told him about her project and requested his help. He said, "Sure. Seems like a good idea to have a history of farm life." He proceeded to tell her how a stockbroker in the town had encouraged him to invest in stocks to supplement his meager farm income.

"He made it sound so good that I mortgaged my farm to buy the stock. The stock failed and we lost the farm. I didn't have any way to pay back the mortgage. So, the bank has taken over the farm."

Meghan asked, "What will you do now?"

The farmer paused and finally said, "I guess I'll have to retire and move to town. I'm discussing with a young couple from the city who are thinking of raising vegetables and flowers on a truck farm on the small acreage around the homestead that we were able to hang onto."

His eyes teared up as he went on, "It was my grandfather's farm that he worked hard for, and made sure he saved enough for taxes. My grandma made enough from her turkeys to pay the taxes during the depression. My parents kept it going during the war. My father once said, 'Funny thing about this country, the only time you can make money is when there's a war'. You just visited the mega-farm down the road? This is how they got the land; they buy it when other farmers can't make a go of it."

Meghan didn't know quite what to say. She told him, "I am so sorry, but perhaps you'd like to make sure your story is included in my documentary." So, she and the recent farmer walked around as he pointed out some interesting aspects of the farm and described his times on the farm with his grandparents and parents.

Meghan was exhausted after these visits. She would finish another day and summarize her findings. She needed to talk to somebody. TJ was the only person she knew at all well around there. They arranged an appointment the next day on the farm which was TJ's responsibility.

Meghan met TJ on the farm. After coffee, Meghan wanted to do some filming of close-ups in the woods. She wanted to show the beauty that binds farm folks to the land. She was filming trees, leaves, tiny flowers on the forest floor, birds, robins and bluebirds, and a squirrel darting about. They heard and saw woodpeckers, but the woodpeckers flew away too fast for her to get a photo.

TJ sat down up against the trunk of a tree. Meghan sat down next to him. She felt his arms and kisses on her lips. Meghan felt her energy spent on her interview experiences with the farmers. She was ready to be held among the wildflowers and wild strawberries. She became overwhelmed by TJ's touch and close body presence. She felt an arm around her and a hand on her thigh. Meghan edged over to his lap.

"Yes?"

"Yes."

With her skirt and underwear down and legs spread, Meghan sat on his lap facing him. She came down on the up-right penis now sticking up out of his jeans. Both cooperated in up and down motions. The larger diameter of the base of the penis was a stimulating bonus in this position for Meghan. Neither were conscious of the woods or the beautiful scenes Meghan had just been photographing.

After much up and down movement, the tension dropped suddenly. Relaxation came and they lingered in the position for a few minutes before Meghan dismounted and they stood up. She put her lips to his with a long kiss. After organizing their appearance, Meghan picked up her camera and they walked out of the woods back to the house. They sat quietly with a glass of wine and a sandwich.

Meghan and TJ gazed at each other with loving expressions. After a long while, Meghan brought up the question of which farms she might visit next. She hoped that the next ones might not be as depressing as the ones she had visited yesterday.

Beth had just gotten back to the book and what she had just read excited her. Meghan's and TJ's love in the woods reminded her of her first experience with her husband, John. They had been wandering the farm that his parents owned and where he had grown up. He planned to take over his parents' farm when he had completed his university studies. Beth and he were both back from their universities' breaks and beginning to think ahead to their futures.

They had recently reconnected, years after getting to know each other briefly during high school. They were falling completely in love. They walked around the wooded pasture and sat down among the trees colored for fall to watch the sunset.

Beth felt his arm around her. They lay on the grass side by side. She heard him say, "You are so beautiful. I love to be close to you." Soon she felt his embrace tighten. She felt him on top of her with their lower clothes off. She felt his hands going over her body and then she felt him inside of her. She felt rhythmic movements up and down. Her body felt more and more excited.

She felt good as he pulled out and they lay together. They got dressed. John kissed and hugged her. Then he said, "This is our secret, OK? My parents wouldn't approve of our use of the woods this way." Winter came by the time he returned from school and so his dad's car's back seat became the setting for love. After savoring the memories of their beginning sex life, Beth read on.

Meghan decided to wait until the next day to continue farm interviews. She and TJ had driven past a prosperous-looking farm that she hoped would provide more cheer than the farms she had just visited. They drove up to the entrance pleasantly lined with pine trees. The house was nearly new and spacious. A big rock with marigolds around it decorated the front yard.

She approached the door where a tall man was standing. Meghan explained her purpose and he agreed to talk to her about his farming experience.

"My father had this farm before me. I had to go to the military but my brother and father carried on. My brother and I continued farming this and a neighboring farm when I returned. Altogether, we have about four hundred acres. We never mortgaged the land and so we have been better off than others around. My wife teaches at the university and our two children are in grade school.

"I met my wife at the Louvre in Paris at a meeting arranged by my niece who was her student. We are probably not typical rural folks but rural communities are more complicated than people think. They are more intertwined with the larger world than years ago. So, the urban-rural split we hear about may be more political perception than reality. We go to the nearby town and even to the Twin Cities often.

"Our lives are busy but happy with normal challenges. We grew potatoes years ago but when that became less profitable, we switched to grain. Less work and more cash. But not all farmers are as well set. I just heard that a neighbor some miles away has killed himself. He went to see the minister and acted as if he would kill the minister but he turned the gun on himself.

"It seems he had financial troubles from buying farms and a grain elevator, all mortgaged and he couldn't make the payments. So, all is not happy in the valley."

Meghan was hearing about the best and the worst extremes of farm stories from the owner of this farm. The potato, now a grain farmer, showed her around the farmstead and pointed out his turning fields of grain. It would soon be harvesting time. Now this was a model farm, one for the photo books with the new house in the old location and a beautiful barn.

Meghan went on to a farm toward the end of the road. The farmstead was fenced with whole trees. She found the owner and asked about the fence.

"My sister did the fencing. She got put in a state hospital."

Whoa, Meghan thought. "One can't be too creative with fencing around here." This farmer was a retired sailor whose parents had come from Norway. He was called Hellesylt named after the town from which his parents had emigrated. His farm was small by today's standards, a hundred and sixty acres. He had a few animals and some crop land. He gestured toward his surrounding land.

He invited Meghan in for pancakes. She was somewhat concerned about the apparent lack of sanitation. The kitchen was tiny and dirty, but she thought pancakes would be OK. He got nicely flowered plates out of the cupboard.

"The chickens aren't laying so there aren't any eggs for the pancakes."

Meghan thought the pancakes would at least be hot, so that would be OK. Coffee would be hot too so that would be OK. She ate the pancakes with Karo syrup. The man picked up the plates and put them on the floor for the cats to lick. Meghan thought, *He will wash them so that should be OK.* Then he picked up the plates, wiped them off with his dirty hanky, and put them back in the cupboard exactly where he had gotten them!

Meghan made a hasty goodbye and headed to another Scandinavian bachelor farmer's farm. He farmed three hundred acres, a little less than three hundred and twenty because the cemetery had a portion of the usual three hundred and twenty. This was a model of a well-cared for farm. After Meghan explained her project, the farmer was willing to proudly show off his farmstead. They walked around the edges of his grain fields. There was a sturdy barn he liked to show off.

"My father had a typical farm raising animals and crops. In those days, they used animal waste for fertilizer. Nowadays without animals, we use some chemicals. We never borrowed money but lived within our means and so we never had the financial problems that some neighbors have."

"What will happen to this farm since you have no children?" Meghan asked.

"A neighbor's son will buy it on time and return here from New York when he can. He will rent out the land and get government program money in the meantime. You know, people with children don't always have any children who want to take over the farm. So, they have decisions to make too."

Meghan headed back to TJ's project farm to discuss her latest farm visits. He was feeding the hogs, so she waited in the car until he finished. They went into the house for coffee. They discussed all the different farm situations that she had visited. They agreed that life on the farm these days was not as idyllic as people might think. "People don't see a clear future," said Meghan while thinking of the large farms absorbing the 'less efficient' small farms.

Meghan told TJ that she was reminded of Edgar Lee Masters' *Spoon River*. "I saw how Christian Dallman's farm, of more than three thousand acres, Swallowed the patch of Felix Schmidt, as a bass will swallow a minnow…"

"No, the picture you are getting doesn't seem so idyllic," TJ said. "It seems that at the university, I wasn't quite getting an accurate picture of current agricultural trends either. People there seemed to be quite accepting of the necessity to get bigger. All the consequences of that policy didn't seem to be considered."

Meghan explained that she was going back to the motel to organize notes and photos. They decided TJ would come into town later for supper. He picked her up at the motel. They came into the local restaurant where they had first met the local farmers days ago. "I have a much better feel for what is happening. I'll be able to put together a media report when I leave here that will explain some of the different urban-rural perceptions of events," Meghan told TJ.

They talked about many things, including their plans, he finishing at the university and then taking over his parents' farm and she about her new faculty position at a university in Minnesota. They were both excited over their new opportunities. But then came the realization of what that meant for them to continue life together. "I've had a wonderful experience with you. I don't want it to end," Meghan said.

TJ leaned across the table. "I know exactly what you mean. I don't want to leave you," TJ said with a serious look on his face.

"I know what you mean. I feel the same. But it's our previous commitments that we must go to when we leave here. We're bound to them," Meghan answered.

TJ quickly agreed. Back at the motel, Meghan sat down on the bed. She saw his tall, large-shouldered body standing over her and felt him slip onto the bed beside her. They started to watch a movie. She felt his embrace. They started removing their clothes, all of them this time. Under the sheets they slipped. She felt TJ embrace her, skin to skin, and touching her all over with kisses. She felt him slip into her smoothly and she felt complete.

The two of them repeated the events of that evening several more times before the day that Meghan had to leave for the final portion of her road trip to her new job. Each time, they clung to each other, not wanting to break the spell. But the day finally came when she had to leave. She had postponed the separation as long as possible. Meghan packed her photo equipment and her clothes.

She looked at the clothes from the wild strawberry patch and smiled. Car was packed, the motor and tires checked, the motel checkout was completed. The time had come to say goodbye, first to the motel manager. Anyone who stays a month in a small-town motel is practically family. The manager had been so happy to know any news Meghan had (that she was willing to give).

Meghan drove out to the farm to say goodbye to TJ. TJ came out of the house. She got out of the car. They embraced for a long time. Neither wanted to pull away. After a half hour, she said, "Thanks for everything. You have my email. Keep in touch." Meghan drove down the driveway to the main road.

She felt sad but also glad. "I got everything I could have wanted here." She tried to get her mind focused on the road first and then her destination. "I will put together my documentary with my next grant installment after I arrive." She felt relaxed and ready to meet new challenges.

Beth had to put down the book. It was time to get her family going for the day. She had gotten up early to get back to the book. She was anxious to see what was going to happen to Meghan. She said to herself, "Meghan's life certainly is proving to be more exciting than my own days. Except for my occasional reading, graphic work, and neighbor visits, including with my in-laws, my days are fairly programmed and similar, day after day. Like Groundhog Day."

Beth had taken the book along to work where she could read for a few minutes at her desk. She was enjoying Meghan's road trip. *I can imagine myself riding along with her*, she thought. "After TJ, what next?" She joined Meghan on the journey as she opened the book to continue reading.

Meghan needed to drive about a thousand miles to get to her school. A constant panoramic of grain crops turned gold and ready for harvesting, wooded hills, farmsteads, and little towns in valleys. Beautiful country, great for a road trip even if it is not strictly for pleasure. The night at a motel had been arranged by her previous motel. A restful but a poignant night alone, and Meghan got on her way. She should arrive at her new school later that day.

Chapter 3
Meghan Settles in at
Her University

The department chair of the Fine Arts department was waiting for her to arrive with a letter which had already arrived for her in his hand. It was from her grant office. She did not open it in front of him. He greeted her warmly. The department chair was glad when Meghan took the position since she had so many qualifications, they could have her handle many tasks. He talked to Meghan about her schedule for the fall term. It looked full.

She was also supposed to direct the fall play as well. She asked about typical schedules and assistants for the play. She found out that she had a typical schedule and she would get student committees for help. The chair took her to HR for payroll and to get other information. Meghan would be able to stay at the dormitory until she found her own apartment. When she and the chair finished with details of the position, the chair invited her for a cup of coffee.

He asked about her project. Meghan excitedly reported on the farms she visited. Meghan told him that "The farm situations reminded her of some of Masters' poems about farm days past. About big farms taking over smaller ones. Not all that seems new is new!"

The chair responded, "As chair in an agricultural region, I have been introduced to *Spoon River*. I agree with your observation. Rural versus urban can be a context for tension here. The university is in a farm belt and the university has an agriculture department so we can't escape that. The rural community is an important constituent group for the college."

Meghan thought, *A point for me.*

Meghan found her temporary housing in the dormitory and moved in her luggage. She pulled out the letter sent to her in the care of the college. It read, *This letter is to inform you that the remainder of your grant for the farm project will no longer be available.*

"What," Meghan said out loud. She immediately called her old graduate school.

The financial official would only say, "The grant remainder has been used for other purposes." She was here, not there, which made resisting the decision difficult. After a period of disappointment, she decided she would make use of her gathered material by creating a different publication with that material.

Meghan knew she would have to publish something before her third-year review which would precede a tenure decision by year seven at the university.

Meghan had met her department colleagues before when she interviewed on campus. She was grateful that one of the women had invited her for dinner when she arrived. Meghan found her new colleague's charming yellow house with blue trim and a white picket fence. Meghan's new friend provided insights, gossip, and advice for the new position. She even described the single men on campus.

Meghan realized that with the schedule that she was given, she would be so busy that she could see that she would not have much time for any of those single men. One of the men mentioned seemed to have an unusual specialty, Sociology of Sex. She couldn't help but wonder what that would be and what kind of research he would be doing.

The next day, Meghan inspected her new work surroundings, her classrooms, and the theater. The fall play had already been chosen by the department the spring before. The play they chose was *Taming of the Shrew*, a play that features a need for male dominance to straighten out a woman. "Whoa, that takes me back to our going-away conversation. How do we handle the play notes for that? Must talk cautiously to a few people here, I guess."

As classes were scheduled to start the following week. Meghan had been working day and night in preparation. Her classes were British Literature, American Film, Film Production, and Freshman Writing. The syllabus for the writing course had been provided for her by the English department so that all sections would be the same.

Meghan got the class in British Literature started. She had included the play that was to be presented that fall. A student raised her hand and asked, "How come we are doing *Taming of the Shrew* this year? Who chose that? That's not going to go over well with people in Women Studies."

Oh, great, Meghan thought. *I'm supposed to defend that.* She answered, "It was chosen by the department before I came. I'll be happy to hear of ideas on how to present that play and the play notes."

Meghan was tired after a week of thesis statements, questions about whether American violence in the streets came from video games and movies, and clarification of syllabus requirements. She told the students that past data showed that American movies are made especially for sixteen- to twenty-five-year-old males. The movies along with war equipment are America's primary exports. She said, "Perhaps you can imagine what impression these exports give of us around the world?"

At the end of the week, the first faculty meeting of the year was scheduled. New faculty are introduced at that time. Based on her observations of styles Meghan had seen on campus the first week, she chose a simple slack outfit. Such an outfit shouldn't be too controversial. All she had to do was stand, smile, and accept applause. *I'll take it*, she thought. *Might be a while before that happens again.*

Various committees reported. Meghan noted that the professor of Sociology of Sex reported on Student Affairs! "Really," she said to herself. "They have a committee for that?" New committees had been elected last spring but new faculty had to be assigned and approved. Meghan was nominated to the Social Committee and the Admissions Committee. *Nothing too controversial there*, she thought. *Also, nothing to rock the boat either. Probably just as well.*

Within two weeks, tryouts for the fall play had to take place. There were only two women, Meghan and another woman who conducted the tryouts after school. Once the actors had been chosen, a meeting of the actors was set for the next week to decide how to characterize the play in the playbill for a modern audience sensitive to women's inequality to men. The actors assembled. By now, they had read the play.

In Shakespeare's play, Katherina was starved, thirsted, and deprived of sleep to get her to comply with her husband's demands. A student reacted, "That's torture," and in a shaking voice asked, "Is torture what Shakespeare called taming?"

Thank you, women's studies student, Meghan thought to herself. Out loud, she said, "Deprivation in that time would probably be considered as 'for her own good', to borrow a title from a book about religion's treatment of women. The treatment elicited behavior that would have made Katherina more fit for the male-dominated culture and, therefore better adjusted. She represented a strong-willed woman, so breaking her 'will' seemed to be the prescription for taming."

Another student who will play Katherina read a quote in which Katherina says, 'My tongue will tell the anger of my heart, or else my heart concealing it will break'.

"So, she wasn't really tamed in the end. She explains that when she responds to orders on demand that she is merely doing her wifely duty, pretending that she has been tamed. Merely adapting to male-structured society," Meghan responded. "This discussion is a big help for relating Shakespeare's time to our own male-structured culture."

Despite Meghan's and the actor's efforts to portray Katherina acceptably to themselves, Katherina's plight began to wear on the actor playing her character. Meghan noticed that the actor seemed detached lately and wondered if something was wrong. *Maybe I have done something*, she thought. She decided to come right out and ask the actor, "Is something happening with you lately? You seem distracted."

At first, the actor said, "Nothing." Meghan waited quietly. Suddenly, the student blurted out, "I'm a women's studies major. I didn't read this play before I auditioned. My big issue is equality for women. This play is horrible. I know it was a different time and torture like this wouldn't be allowed today, but there is still so much evidence around us of sexism and male culture.

"Just pick up a newspaper, about two women a month are killed by their men in our state! Duty to men continues on to this day. My grandma told me about duty. Grandpa chaired an anti-abortion meeting in their living room. Grandma didn't sit with them in the meeting. She said that it was her duty to make coffee as a wife but she wouldn't sit in there with those at the meeting, which, of course, included her husband."

Meghan tried to think fast. "You are right, but you are not Katherina. She and you are messengers for Shakespeare who was trying to tell an audience how far denying women personhood could go in the name of society which sees women as property. It is an old message from long ago, but the message is still relevant today. We can hope that there will be people in the audience who may be helped to see this reality around them or even realize we have a message for them that we think they are being mistreated."

Katherina's impersonator listened carefully. She wanted to believe Meghan. "OK, I will think about what you are saying. I know I made a commitment and I need to carry it out. I will try to be a messenger, not a person who believes in this kind of treatment for a woman." And so, play practice with Katherina went on.

Beth had to stop reading after this section. She said to herself, "I've heard of this play, *Taming of the Shrew*, but I've never heard of torture as the method of taming. Good grief, what next? Taming by torture? It should be illegal. It's abuse, for sure. People have beaten children and animals. I suppose beating a wife also has been acceptable. It shouldn't be but it must have been acceptable in Shakespeare's time.

"I'm glad I don't have to live with that. That's a low standard for a husband, but we have to be grateful for all things, I suppose. Beating and hitting at all should certainly be considered assault and therefore be illegal. I've heard that even spanking children is illegal in some countries. It is illegal in schools in many states in this country. I can't believe any of this. Poor Meghan, how's she going to explain this? I feel like protesting myself." After that internal verbal outburst, Beth picked up the book again.

The set and lighting committees had joined the group. Most had been involved in school plays before and knew their way around the set materials and costumes they had available. These were noted and lists of additional needs were constructed.

The play was a huge success. Many in the audience stayed to visit with Meghan and the assistant director afterward, including faculty and community members. The sociologist on sexology complimented her on her work. It would make sense that he would take an interest in the play for two reasons, the topic and Meghan herself. She was the new attractive faculty member at a school that seemed not to have too much new going on at any given time.

The reviews were excellent. They gave Meghan a 'Bravo' for avoiding a gender war. A letter to the editor wrote that the approach was too feminist, but that was about the only criticism. The playbill announced the date for a panel presentation on 'Cultural Analysis of Gender Roles' later in the term.

Meghan didn't get enough time off for a Thanksgiving trip home. She was invited to her colleague's apartment for that holiday. She had regularly called her parents during the fall. They all planned for a Christmas celebration at the end of the term. Work had been so demanding that Meghan had little time to look for an apartment for herself. Her colleagues had been helping her by watching and listening to places for rent.

When she does find an apartment, Meghan will have to look at thrift stores for furniture, no Ikea around here.

At the dorm, there was little privacy as the students were so sociable with her, maybe because she was so close to some of their ages herself. Some of them chatted with her as if they were close friends. For example, how else would she know that some of the women students compete to see how far they can thrust hard-boiled eggs from their vaginas. She didn't exactly get that but listened intently to their discussions.

The time in the term came to plan for the Martin Luther King celebration in January. A committee was formed consisting of faculty, which included Meghan, and student representatives. It was important to honor the date this year, especially because the school had not done so last year. One of the students reported that she had overheard some students discussing that announcement. One student challenged the whole idea with, "Why do we have to do something special that day? We don't have any black students here."

"That's not the point," the committee member reported having informed that student. "MLK Day is for our whole country. A reminder of what he tried to tell Americans—his dream—that it is the character of the person not the skin color that is the basis for judging others. It is a good time to go over the point that the history of the U.S. is one history of all its people, and all are participants in that history. Besides, how do you know that we have no students of color here? Maybe they are just not dark enough for your category?"

Of course, the rest of the committee agreed with her, or they likely wouldn't have agreed to be on the committee. Another member spoke up saying, "We will need a black speaker."

"What? No, it's the ideas, not the color! We shouldn't have to have a black person tell whites or even worse ask whites for understanding. Somehow that doesn't seem a right thing to ask."

The chair intervened to keep the group on task. "Well, we're not ruling any idea out yet. Let's make a list of possible speakers and then discuss what we have. This celebration is for America, everybody."

"A local minister. The one with the sign, 'Black Lives Matter'."

"Quotes from Langston Hughes 'Let America be America again'."

"That's too depressing, it just describes what is, doesn't point to hope enough."

The chair again said, "We are just making a list now. We'll save our comments until we run out of ideas for our list."

"How about Martin Luther King's actual speech? A reading of it or maybe a video of MLK giving his speech or an excerpt of it?"

"Amanda Gorman's *The Hill We Climb* is a poem of hope for us all. An excerpt of that might be good." After the committee gave a few more ideas, the chair suggested they vote. She handed out slips of paper for writing their favorite ideas. A video excerpt of Martin Luther King himself and an excerpt of Amanda Gorman's poem read by an English professor were the ideas with the most votes.

The committee will ask an English professor to select an excerpt and a student speaker to read the excerpt. The music department will decide on music and musicians for the program. The meeting concluded with the plan and a thank you from the chair.

Meghan mostly listened in the MLK committee meeting. Now that play season was over for Meghan, she was feeling more sociable and she was gradually getting acquainted with various professors. One day, she stopped by the faculty coffee lounge a few minutes before the crowd arrived. Martin, the sociologist, walked in and offered to bring her coffee. She noticed his smile and friendly manner. Meghan responded with a friendly smile and a thank you.

They became engaged in a discussion about the latest administrative announcement regarding the college budget. They recognized the problem but didn't get anywhere near solving it, so they went on to get more acquainted with each other.

Meghan and Martin talked about where they grew up and had gone to college. Martin seemed kind enough and he was certainly handsome enough. Meghan looked forward to talking to him again. She even tried to come early to coffee hour whenever she could and so did he. They talked about classes, current events, the arts, and the college topics of the day. She asked him about his specialty, Sociology of Sex. He related the topic to the larger picture of gender in society without many specifics.

Meghan pointed out, "The arts world also is part of that whole picture. Literature often can be pretty pointed in its expositions of human behavior without surveys and experiments, just with careful observation."

Beth hated to interrupt her reading, just as she was suspecting a relationship was developing between Meghan and Martin. She had to work on her graphics. Beth noted that academic settings seemed to have issues like those she found in business situations. Both have organizational and management problems with prejudices that interfere with smooth operations. Even the urban-rural perceptual differences seemed to come up in colleges in rural areas.

Challenges everywhere. She was way into the book and was still wondering about the connection between people in her area and this book. She also hoped the pace of the book would pick up soon as some of those committee meetings go so slowly, but she supposed she was getting an honest picture. She imagined, though, "Such smart folks should be able to be more efficient than what she had seen at her workplace and in her community."

Beth had to put in her quota of time parent helping at the co-op preschool. So, she could not get back to the book for several days. She was anxious to get back to the possible romance of Meghan and Martin, so she began reading early in the morning before the family was up.

One day, Martin came by early and so did Meghan. Quickly before anyone else came, he invited her to dinner and a high school play in a neighboring town during the following week. Meghan thought, *Why not? I've heard nothing from TJ.* She had hoped for a little communication, but "I guess that I didn't really expect to hear from him."

"That would be very nice," Meghan responded. "I like your idea of the neighboring town. Sometimes life can feel a little close here."

The next week, they arrived at the restaurant, a classier one than any in their college town. A glass of wine and talking came easier without the watchful eyes of other faculty, staff, and students. They both tried to avoid work talk, though it was not easy. They talked about their academic fields and what they hoped to achieve within them. Meghan teased him a little about being a subject in his own research.

Martin blushed and responded, "No, I'm not a modern Kinsey. There is already a lot of research in that area. I'm especially interested in how sex and gender interact within social classes such as male dominance in power structures and relationships. That kind of information can be obtained through interviews and surveys." She felt his hand over hers and she left it there. She probably wasn't likely to be a participant in his research but maybe there would be other possibilities.

They finally got up to leave to get to the play on time. *Our Town* is a play presented over and over in high schools, especially in small towns. The acting is mostly what differentiates one presentation from another. It's hard to make a set of people sitting in chairs too unique. Meghan didn't want to be too critical as Martin had chosen the evening's entertainment.

They settled down into their chairs. Meghan sensed the excitement in the theater that is always present moments before a play starts. Absorbed by the actors' performances, Meghan could still feel his hand holding hers. She didn't move it.

After the numerous curtain calls, a greeting or two from several audience members, Meghan and Martin walked to his car. Meghan mentioned that when she first saw the play as a younger girl, "I was annoyed by the play." They continued the conversation as they rode back to the university.

"Why? It has always seemed to me to be emphasizing that we should value each day," Martin argued.

"Yes, but no matter how mundane? It seemed to me to be small-town boring. How do you value each day then?" Meghan said curtly.

"Some of the community members in *Our Town* didn't seem so happy with the place in their town either. Two committed suicide. Maybe it's just an observation of how life goes," Martin said, as he attempted to de-escalate the conversation.

"Yes, and how does it go? To just observe is to accept. People must fit into other people's worlds, not their own. They must lower their aspirations to fit. The couple didn't feel they were ready to get married but they did anyway. They are bound, wings clipped before they have a chance to fly."

"Well, maybe the script is trying to tell us to value each day but maybe the town doesn't give people enough reason to appreciate that idea," Martin said as he searched for a compromise view.

They chatted about how enjoyable the evening was on the way to her dorm. In front of the door, she turned, felt his hand on her arm, and heard his good night wish as he turned toward his car. "All perfectly proper," she said to herself. "Maybe too proper, but one can't be too proper here, I suppose."

Chapter 4
Experts Describe Men's World

Now the panel program date that had been announced on the university playbill was looming. Meghan had been asked to convene a committee and function as moderator for the evening. *Being a moderator shouldn't be too controversial*, Meghan thought to herself. "There are lots of cultural and emotional layers involved in these gender topics."

The committee met and chose Martin to give a presentation on the topic, 'The Male Dominant Culture and Its Effects'. A second talk would be, 'The Me Too Movement for Credentials'. Martin agreed to prepare a talk and elicit discussion. They would have to look for another panelist for the talk on downgrading women's credentials to maintain dominance and pay women less than men. Where to get such a person? The committee thought it should be a woman, from off campus.

In the meantime, Martin would occasionally bounce ideas off Meghan regarding the panel. Meghan had many ideas as she hearkened back to the women's discussion that last evening at graduate school. One day in the coffee room, Meghan brought up the panel. "You know, the U.S. is a white male culture, right?" She was pushing him a bit to think about the topic, as well as testing his thinking on the topic.

"I know there are gender differences in our culture but that's two sub-cultures. Are you saying the whole culture is white male?" Martin asked.

"Yes, it is the dominant culture. Women's culture exists within white male culture. So do ethnic cultures," responded Meghan.

Martin questioned, "I know that our country is considered a 'masculine' culture compared to other cultures. It's also considered a patriarchal culture. But white male? My mother ran our home show and so do all in my background. So, I don't know."

"Yeah, does a fish know water? I know it can seem like moms run the show. She is usually the home organizer but that doesn't mean she oversees the culture. In fact, women and ethnic groups know white males better than white males know themselves because those groups must maneuver within the white male culture," Meghan pointed out.

Another man who had just entered the room spoke up. "Oh, it's women who run our schools and homes."

"Oh, oh," Meghan realized. "Time for me to get back to my office hour."

"I'll walk out with you," said Martin. "You were going to leave me with that guy?"

"Sure, it was sounding as if you would agree with him."

"How about meeting after work for coffee? I'll stop by your office."

At the coffee house, Martin came armed with examples to use for argument against Meghan's comments. "What about a guy kneeling on this knee proposing? Doesn't that suggest women's power over men?"

"OK, it does look like that, doesn't it? But if we think of the totality of gender relationships, the idea is that he is still picking her, isn't it? She is supposed to pick from the men who show interest in her. Oh, I know there are cues she can give about her likelihood of agreeing, but the guy is still supposed to do the picking. That's a part of courting behavior. Promises are made but often behavior tends to change after marriage."

"Yes, I suppose you are right about that. How about some of those cues?" Martin joked.

"OK, you're kidding, right? We're talking about a panel here. But let's change the subject. It's a wonderful day today for walking along the river and forgetting about anything connected with work." Meghan didn't bring up the panel again but she did tell him about some of the remarks from her friends about unequal power in relationships back at the university on her last day there.

It was soon time for Christmas vacation. Meghan flew home to her family ranch in Nebraska. She had a great time helping trim the tree and preparing the special Christmas breads and other special food. The house was filled with relatives on Christmas Day. Everybody was excited to see each other apart from Uncle Don who kept wanting to get the topic on to politics and his point of view.

Meghan thought, *who wants to talk about how awful the federal government is on Christmas? I know the feds want to raise your grazing rent, but hey, it's Christmas!*

During the break, Meghan was able to rent an apartment because some students managed to get into school housing which opened an apartment. Meghan wanted private housing with more privacy away from campus and groups of walking students. She found a basement apartment with a fireplace. She would now be able to invite Martin over for dinner sometime.

But before that could happen, she would ask if he would help her move her things over to the apartment. She had bought a few pieces of furniture. She thought, *why are men dominant in all cultures?* She asked students that once. After a long pause, a guy had said tentatively, 'Because they're stronger?'. "So, time for Martin to come through with an excuse for dominance. (But we have machines now, brains are equivalent.)"

When they met in the coffee room after vacation, Meghan told him about her new place and asked if he would help her make the move. By using both cars, they could accomplish the move after school and before dinner. After moving her things in, they went for an early supper at a local cafe. Some students, who were also having a good time there, noticed them and waved. They whispered among themselves a little and then went on with their own good time.

Students often know teachers only in class and can be surprised to see them in civilian life. It can be a big shock to see them downtown in shorts, for example. Small-town universities are more accustomed to seeing faculty outside of class, but seeing a man and a woman teacher together does make for some talk. This will be over much of the school by tomorrow.

Meghan and Martin talked about mundane school topics such as parking lot rules for faculty and students. Martin gave her some history. "We used to have our own individual spots with our names on headstones and the school provided that as a free benefit for faculty. Now the parking spots in the lots are hundreds of dollars a year. We didn't necessarily get raises to cover that, so there went a perk. We still don't have enough parking spaces for all who have paid, so looking for a parking spot is called a lottery by the faculty."

"No wonder parking is one of the main issues on campuses," Meghan said. "You'd wish it would be something loftier, wouldn't you?"

"Well, I guess it encourages one to find other means of getting here," said Martin.

A couple of weeks later, Meghan put a note in Martin's PO box with an invitation to dinner on the following Friday evening. Martin responded with a note accepting.

Meghan checked to make sure the fireplace was working. Imagine smoke all over. She got the OK from the landlord, so she got some birch logs. She also bought Almadine Rose wine since she usually didn't keep alcohol on hand. During the afternoon, Meghan set table settings with flowers in front of the fireplace, prepared a chicken dinner, and lit the fireplace. She thought, *A beautiful setting if I say so myself.*

Martin arrived. He looked impressed. "This is beautiful. The apartment has come a long way since we brought your things over. And a fire. So pleasant and cozy."

"Have a chair," Meghan gestured. She served Martin a glass of wine and poured one for herself. They sat in front of the fire, a little hypnotized by the flames. After a half hour, Meghan got up to serve the meal, and they both sat down at the table. "This meal is wonderful," Martin said.

"Just look, you've roasted a whole chicken, baked potatoes with butter, and cooked asparagus. It's so nice of you to do this and the Danish dessert looks delicious."

They talked about many topics, politics, their families (she didn't dare tell him yet about Uncle D and his messianic politics), and not about work at all. They moved to easy chairs in front of the fire. As the fire was burning down. Martin announced, "I'd better get going. It's getting late."

Meghan responded, "Yes, we both have papers this time of the term. We've had a wonderful time." She walked him to the door. Martin stood and held her for a very long time, probably a half hour at least. She reached up and kissed him goodbye. "See you tomorrow," she said in response to his goodbye.

Meghan had various preparations for spring term classes. The class on art and social issues could get some pushback from some of the students. She chose several paintings to illustrate her social issue choices. Two important issues she selected were 'Anno Domini B 52' and 'The Crowning'. The anti-war painting presented a B 52 bomber in the shape of Jesus on the cross. 'The Crowning' pictures a baby's head coming out of the birth canal.

The latter was presented as a part of the women's movement which promoted the importance and equal worth of women. Gender roles also appeared in *The Rape of Europa* which depicts Europa as a beautiful woman goddess and the god Jupiter as a white bull. The painting by Titian symbolized the effort of a man changing his appearance to endear himself to a woman and then taking the opportunity to rape her.

This painting by Titian is a late 1300 A.D. representation of human behavior and gender inequality from a myth that dates even farther back in Greek mythology.

Meghan was surprised that the students approached the paintings as a representation of history, so therefore, not representing today's world. Since the issues weren't current, apparently, they were not threatening. On the other hand, the students couldn't see any relationship to their current culture either. "You don't see any relationship to our current culture? Let's look at the military budget.

"Locations of our troops around the world, our way of handling issues through force. No relationship? Are women making as much money as men now?"

"OK, they could see some relationships to the present if I put it that way. But they would rather think that all such issues were in the past. Surely, these problems would have been resolved by now. Anyway, we are not in a war now. Women are doing well now," the students agreed.

Maybe, Meghan thought. "They are right, maybe we continue to fight our own past issues when they have been settled. But maybe the issues are still here in different wrappings, festering and waiting for an excuse to burst out. Women are still getting paid about twenty percent less than men."

She told the students, "I remember my professor talking about a political survey given forty years ago. The dominant three issues that led to the survey were abortion, guns, and homosexuals (not marriage, seemingly just the right to exist). Sometimes our culture changes little, sometimes a lot, and sometimes not at all if you look over the long term.

Meghan mentioned that sometimes important issues come and go.

"For example, When I was in college, we had the first Earth Day. A few years later, it had morphed into Keg Day. Did our environmental problems go away?" She thought, *Tomorrow, I will ask the students what issues they see now.*

"What do you see as your big issues of the day?" Meghan asked the students the next day. They answered, marijuana and other drugs, mass shooters, student loans, sustainability, and reproduction. Meghan agreed that these are important issues. She listened and asked what kind of art could express these issues. The students got an assignment to express one of their issues in an art piece.

The students turned in their issues-themed art works. There were several that related to each of the following examples. Street gun fights were the topic with several variations. One drawing had a group of youths with guns pointed at another group across the street which also had guns pointed back toward them. Another painting featured a group of children on the floor in a circle looking up at a teacher.

A statement in a circle above stated, *Miss Mary, we have a plan. If there is a shooter, we will go under the stairs, not where the loudspeaker says, the shooter will know where we are then.* Some other art also showed school shooters.

Some young women had produced art involving protest marches regarding the abortion controversy. Women were carrying signs with messages such as, 'My body, my business', and 'Government, leave my body alone', and related messages. There was one showing a bloody fetus.

The art works summarized the disagreement within society about the reach of government over reproductive issues.

One drawing represented students with college loans. A male student had a student loan bill of $60,000 in one hand and job ads in another with the question below, 'How?'.

Several students had produced art illustrating global climate change effects. One painting was mostly fire with some dried brown evergreens in the forefront about to be devoured by the fire. Another showed a melting glacier running water into the ocean. Another showed Florida flooding. Other art showed waste piles such as piles of plastic objects and bags, smokestacks with black smoke, and car traffic gridlock. There was even a photo of cows with the words 'Methane producers' for the caption.

All in all, the art did not indicate indifferent, happy-go-lucky students, but students with many concerns about their futures. Meghan decided that they all needed some time to label and discuss their fears and to look for hope. She had them discuss where they saw hope. Some said they had some hope that governments would respond to their concerns. They could vote for candidates who listed remedies on their platforms.

They could use social and political pressure and consumer pressure on corporations to mend their ways. A few students who had taken environmental studies brought up instances of improvement in water quality such as 'Unsafe for Human Contact' signs taken up from the upper Mississippi years ago (It was now safe to swim.), the return of the eagles and the increasing efforts to preserve habitat.

They could look at their own consumption habits in relation to the global need for change, drive less, no plastic bags, and other energy consumption and waste habits. "Just doing something can make us less fearful," Meghan told the students. This had been an emotionally expressive assignment but put Meghan and the students in the same place.

The date for the panel on culture was approaching. Meghan was concerned about preparations. She was growing anxious about Martin's preparation as he had not mentioned anything about working on his panel presentation. She finally came right out and asked him, "Are you working on your panel presentation? I'm not trying to be pushy, but yes, I am trying to nudge you to get going on it. Remember I'm going to be the moderator."

"Yes, I have outlined the topics at least," Martin answered. "I plan to spend this weekend on whatever research I need to complete the presentation. Then I can get you an outline."

Meghan went on to explain why she seemed so concerned. "Once I presented an analysis of a Spanish novel, with the theme of gender, to the participants of a faculty retreat. I presented a careful psychological analysis of gender issues in the novel. A male faculty member also had been asked to speak on the novel. He got up in front of the group, hands in his pockets, jingling his keys and coins, and discussed his relationship with his wife. Winging it, no evidence of any preparation at all!

"There was supposed to be a discussion after each presentation. Not one word from the faculty audience after my presentation. Dead silence. After the winging male presentation, lively discussion. One female faculty monopolized the discussion. I never attended another faculty retreat. So, I don't want a repeat of that in this panel."

Martin responded, "No, no, I'll treat it as a class lecture. I'll be prepared, I'll give you an outline ahead of time."

Two weeks later, Meghan inquired of Martin and the committee about their plans. The committee had hired a human resources consultant from a feminist employment agency for the topic of downgrading women's credentials to fit the dominant culture. Meghan explained to the committee and Martin the procedure that she planned to follow.

"A week before I want outlines from each panelist who will have fifteen minutes to make a presentation. Then, I will open it up for discussion from the audience. After both presentations and discussions, I will give a short summary." It appeared that the panel preparations were on track.

The evening of the panel arrived. Meghan introduced herself and the panel, Professor Martin, and Dr. Golden. Golden worked on placing women professionals in positions and sometimes counseling those already on the job. Professor Martin Fitjar was introduced as a specialist in culture and gender relationships. Meghan took notes on what the speakers said. The notes would help her as moderator of the panel.

Three points were projected in front of the room: Male Dominance, Women as Property, and Courting Culture. Martin began with a question. "According to anthropologists, males are dominant in all cultures. Can we think of any reason that might be the case?"

Quiet audience. Finally, an older woman spoke up, apparently to make a point and to inject some humor, said, "For sure, it's not that they have more brains!"

A guy suggested, "Because they are bigger and stronger?"

Martin responded, "As a matter of fact, both of you are on to something here. In earlier times, strength was an important factor, I'm sure. But in today's world, more emphasis is on brain work. This makes it possible to construct a culture of equality. But we do need to start with a very old concept that women are property. There have been regular inroads to this idea such as women now being able to have charge accounts, property, and loans in their names.

"But women are still property when dealing with the sexual territory. They are restricted from being in control of their own bodies. Restricted from abortions and even contraception in some cases. Restrictions are allowed at drug stores if the clerk says a sale is against his religion. The clerk may be able to refuse a sale of contraceptive items.

"Companies or agencies which have people who say these services are against their values may be allowed to refuse reproductive services in the health insurance they offer, though the law requires these services. We see continual political efforts in most states and some courts in the U.S. to further restrict women in these areas. Not only can they be restricted by individual men but also by society in general.

"For example, a judge stated that 'when a woman lies with a man, her body becomes public property'.

"I'm sure you've heard the saying, 'It's a man's world'. Let's see to what extent that is so. We don't even have much for names for women's bodies' reproductive parts that aren't male-oriented. Women have a sub-culture which is an adjunct to male culture. This sub-culture may include some in-home decisions. This women's role has developed as an adaptation to the dominant male culture.

"Women are expected to yield to men, even when walking down the street. In politics, how many times have you heard a woman running for public office say, 'I'm not a feminist'. They must reassure men that they know their place. We have heard many times, 'I'm not a feminist, but I want equal pay for equal work'. Again, ingratiating men."

Martin went on. "So, you think that a woman gets to decide to marry a certain man? But custom has him asking her to marry him. Yes, there is a brief sojourn into what seems like giving women more power. I quote a woman's comment, 'They have to make a big deal of the wedding because that's all there is'. As a part of courting, men make promises.

"This is courting behavior and tends to drop off soon after the wedding. They never intended to keep the courting promises (Even at the wedding, the woman promises to obey the husband). Then they go right back into male culture. Many women can give you examples of this. When the wedding of two professional people was over, one husband said to his bride, 'Everything has been your way so far, now everything is going to be my way'. The marriage didn't last, no surprise."

"Thank you, Martin, you have given us much to think about. We will wait for discussion until after both presentations. Now we will hear from Dr. Golden on 'Downgrading Women's Credentials'." Meghan gestured to her to begin. Three points were projected at the front of the room: 'Me Too Movement', 'Male Dominance at Work', and 'Denigration of Women's Credentials and Contributions'.

"I suppose you all have heard of the 'Me Too Movement'. This referred to the escalation of complaints regarding unwanted touching extending to rape in offices, agencies, and institutions. A few women spoke up and even sued and then more and more said, 'Me Too'. From a woman's point of view, these incidents represent women as 'prey' for predatory men.

"Women hadn't even told each other about these types of incidents, tending to blame themselves. They were embarrassed. Not knowing how frequently others were having similar experiences, they tended to keep their experiences to themselves. They had ample experiences with the inability to change the situation, as they were not believed or the people in charge minimized the assaults.

"More likely the women who complained would get fired and the men often avoided any repercussions. So, who is likely to complain under such circumstances? These assaults are not a new phenomenon but the attention being given to them in our society is new. Sometimes these aggressions remain in the thoughts and conversations of men.

"For example, a group of faculty men would meet over beers every Friday afternoon, and among other topics discussed were what the women faculty would look like without clothes! But that is not the main thrust of my talk here today.

"There is another type of attack on women that also is not new. In the past, personal attacks on femininity or attractiveness were common. 'She looks like a man'; 'How could I have raped her, she's too ugly'; or 'She's not my type'; 'She doesn't act like a proper woman'; 'She is arrogant, abrasive, obstreperous'.

"A letter to the editor critical of a previous woman writer, brought on comments such as, 'You must be fat and ugly'; 'You must be on welfare'. The previous writer had not addressed an issue that should elicit such an unrelated response.

"I am not minimizing the above issues in any way. But I want to stress that today we need to move on to denounce the approach that men's dominance behavior has developed since attacks on femininity haven't been as effective in controlling women as they once were. Women must be made aware of their subordinate status at work. Some religions, including some forms of American Christianity, go so far as to say that no man should work under a woman.

"Here are some examples of uncalled for denigration that women have reported from work. Media has its own problems ignoring competence and credentials. Years ago, a television station terminated an attractive forty-year-old woman (a co-anchor) on the basis that she was not deferential enough to the male anchor. Recently, a television commentator suggested that a female running for president was past her prime as women are by fifty.

"This comment was about a woman who had been a governor and an ambassador. The comment was surely an example of denigrating credentials and looking at the woman as a sex object instead of a competent woman.

"A forty-eight-year-old female professional musician who had played countless times over years at a church for weddings, holidays, and other functions came to meet the new Director of Music to introduce herself. His response was, 'We only hire professional musicians'.

"A relatively new Academic Dean told a female senior full professor in a discussion, 'You don't know what you are doing anyway'.

"A faculty woman was told that her degree wasn't from as prestigious a school as that of a comparable man when she asked why she was not paid the same as he was.

"A woman with a Ph.D. went to work for a large corporation. She was put to work making copies. When she questioned if that was the best place for her, she was told, 'All our girls start here'. This placement, by the way, was done by a woman supervisor who had learned well how to function in the male world.

"Research has shown that the prestige of the school a woman graduates from is not a factor in the position she gets. But for men, graduating from a prestigious school assures them of prestigious positions. There are other ways male dominance is expressed at work. A male faculty member ordered me, a senior woman, to make photocopies. I looked surprised but did do it since I had done the original work that the department was using. Later, the man asked me whom I would obey."

Dr. Golden continued, "I want to tell you a story that one of my clients told me. She said, 'When I was in fourth grade, I suddenly sensed a black cloud on my shoulders. I realized that I was a girl and that was not going to be good. This may have been a reaction to the teacher's response to a boy in the room that I sensed was very different from the way she treated me.

"'I assumed I could achieve my way out of girlhood and get on an equal footing with boys and men. I was wrong'. She continued her story into adulthood. 'I did achieve valedictorian in high school (despite being told that those of us from the farms could expect B's if we had gotten A's previously), high academic honors in college, a Ph.D. (the first in my organization), mentions in various *Who's Who* biographies, but in the end, I was not able to achieve my way out of womanhood.

"'I was still a woman in my organization. The one aspect that I could not do with achievement was to be a man, I was still a woman in a male-dominated culture. I was hired in an organization where I organized a department. After the first year, I was asked if I wanted to go on half-time. My response was that it seemed as if people who were paid part-time had to work full-time for part-time pay, so I said "no".

'After two years with the title "acting head" of my department, I said that my status had to be changed as I didn't see any effort to replace me and that it looked like I wasn't going to be the real head. That was changed, I was named "Chair" of my department, but six years later when a male was added, he was given my role as head of the department'."

Dr. Golden's client continued, "'Male colleagues could ignore my comments in meetings or my greetings in the halls, they could put down my questions, give orders (even if less seniority), give no credence to my credentials that should at least make me equal (if not superior), label me as "arrogant", "aggressive", "obstreperous", though I always carefully worded remarks and often served as mediator which seemed to be my assigned role.

"'That didn't leave me with the right to an opinion. I looked for slivers of a silver lining to the black cloud that fell on me as a fourth grader. I pushed it above my shoulders but I have not eliminated it. I am reminded of my friend, also holder of a Ph.D. and work experience at that level, who once said plaintively, "Why am I always a beginner?".'

"This story tells us about the personal experience of the effects of denigration of female credentials, a way of keeping women in their place, lower than male colleagues in our male-dominated culture which includes organizational cultures.

"A man said to a woman, 'You think like a woman!'. We know what that is supposed to imply. Nearly all these comments are expressions of male dominance downgrading women's credentials in the workplace. This downgrading can be used to justify lower pay for women as well as not recognizing women's contributions and sometimes even taking credit for them. How could a woman get credit if she is not capable of doing the work in the first place?

"A college president came to a gathering of alumni for a fund-raising evening. When he entered the room, he uttered in surprise, 'There's just a bunch of women here!'. Yes, a bunch of women college graduates of his institution, many of them widows with money to donate.

"Women are often put in charge of training younger men into their jobs. The men then become the supervisors of the women who trained them! This illustrates the importance of being male. All these experiences, whether of the 'me-too' variety or the denigration of women's credentials, are all oriented toward making sure women know their lesser place.

"It should not be necessary to legislate or regulate relations between men and women in the workplace if the male culture did not objectify women as lesser sex objects. If male culture recognized the equality, importance, achievements, and contributions of women, I guess it wouldn't be the same male culture, would it? And that would be an improvement for women in the workplace."

Meghan thanked the panelists and opened the discussion to the audience for questions and comments.

Comments and questions included the following:

"Women are used to this and some like it the way it is."

Martin responded with, "Yes, you have a point. People are accustomed to the way it is and have come to expect it. Women can feel free even when they have been trained to be subordinated. They may even identify with aggressors. 'He hit me, but I was arguing'. They may be critical of women who want change."

"How do you see male culture being modified?"

Dr. Golden answered, "Gradually, piecemeal, with laws, regulations, discussion, education. We may be so used to the current scene that we don't realize there is a problem until someone points it out. Then we need to act and maintain the new changes. There have been ups and downs historically. In the 1930s, it seemed women were gaining some freedoms, but then with the war and the 50s the country became more gender restricted.

"There were more women doctors in the early 1900s than in 1960. A women's rights movement began in the late 60s among middle class women in the suburbs with restricted possibilities beyond caring for husbands and children. A woman told me that in the late 50s when she took doctoral exams, there were thirty-one men and two women.

"She went to graduate classes for new faculty, the membership included her and forty-eight men along with a nun and an accompanying nun. We can't be doing this sort of thing every generation or so over and over."

"Whatever happened to the ERA?"

Martin answered, "The Equal Rights Amendment needed to pass in three-fourth of the states but it came up a couple of states short. It was opposed by some women and that didn't help. The opposition argued that women might be drafted. Now there is no draft and there are many women in the military. There is talk of resurrecting the ERA again. It was a simple statement of equality. It was not declaring that there was no difference between men and women."

"Can't women control their treatment by how they act and dress?"

Dr. Golden answered, "Sometimes to a degree, but it is difficult to re-direct men's detrimental behavior when it starts. Research has demonstrated that dress isn't correlated with attacks in a general way. If discriminatory behavior is allowed in the workplace, it can become part of the system and difficult to challenge without women facing further discrimination and even termination."

There seemed to be no further questions from the audience, so Meghan directed people toward coffee. There were some bursts of discussion here and there as people stood up and drifted toward the refreshments.

The campus newspaper reported on the events. There were letters to the editor on some of the same topics as the questions. After a few days, the discussions on women became less frequent.

School continued in the usual way with athletic tournaments and other activities. Martin and Meghan talked often and met occasionally in the town.

Beth looked up from the book and gazed into space. *Am I in the same country?* she thought. "I have been going along, tending to business, doing what I and others expected of me without noticing the larger picture. But I'm concerned for my little girl. What is she going to run into as she grows up? Reading about how other women see their world makes me concerned for her.

"It looks like my boy will live in a different world though the world may look the same on the outside. I am really upset by this book but I will keep reading it, if for no other reason to see what it is that people seem to be whispering about. So far, I can't figure it out." She laid the book down for now as her family was waiting for her to go to town where there was an ice cream social. *That will cheer me up,* Beth thought.

Beth and her family had a good time at the park. She didn't get back to the book until the weekend while the children napped. She glanced at the page ahead and saw that Meghan and Martin were leaving town. *This promises excitement,* Beth thought as she began reading.

Chapter 5
Meghan and Martin Look Ahead

Martin's friend was having a book signing in the Twin Cities and Martin asked Meghan if she would like to go. She agreed. It would give her a chance to be with Martin out of sight of the school and town. They decided to get two hotel rooms.

Martin's friend, Paul Keith, had gotten his book published titled, *A Farm Boy's Off-Grid Exploits*. He was signing copies of his book at a local bookstore. Meghan and Martin had brought a copy of the book for him to sign and stood in the line for his signature. When he signed their book, they all agreed to meet after the signing for lunch where Martin and Meghan reviewed their favorite stories from the book with the author.

They recounted the story about raising crows. Paul, being the youngest of the three boys, was charged with climbing the seventy-five-foot-high spruce tree to steal the not fledged young crows to drop them down to the two brothers. The crows were fed with chicken feed mash on a stick. They would hungrily eat the mash off the sticks. Paul and one brother decided to teach the crows to fly.

They tossed the fledglings between them. The crows did not like it. As they grew older and could fly, they avoided the two brothers but enjoyed the oldest brother's company. They would land on his shoulder and steal food from his mouth. The crows would also enjoy themselves harassing the goats and dogs. The crows also had a bad habit of harassing the boys' mother. When she hung out the clothes washing, they would land on the clothesline with their muddy claws and steal the clothes pins.

Paul also had a bottle lamb that had been rejected by its mother. Every morning when Paul got up, he fed the lamb a bottle of warm milk. As the summer progressed, they became good friends. As summer turned to fall, all the lambs were rounded up and loaded into a truck to be shipped to the stockyards to be sold to butchers. Paul's lamb was a quarter mile away eating grass in a ditch. The grownups were unable to catch it.

Paul's dad offered him a dollar if he would call it. Paul refused. After some negotiation, Paul was offered two dollars. He called it and the lamb came running to its doom. Paul said that when he recounted that story to his grandsons many years later, the younger grandson said, 'You shouldn't have called it'.

On another occasion, Paul and his oldest brother went exploring along with several neighborhood boys. It was a hot day and the boys were thirsty, so they stopped at an abandoned farmstead where they saw a water pump. They pumped the handle and sure enough water came out. One of the boys would pump the handle while each boy would cup his hands to catch the water and sip it out of their cupped hands.

After they all had finished drinking, one of the boys lifted a rotten plank that was covering the well. He gave a loud gasp, so the boys all looked into the well to see what he had seen. There were several large bloated dead mice floating on the surface. Again, when Paul said that he recounted that story to his grandsons, the younger boy again commented on the story. He said, 'You shouldn't have looked'.

Paul was known in the neighborhood for being interested in and capable of catching skunks. However, he didn't know how to do it without getting squirted. It took a long time to get rid of the smell. Baths didn't help. He had heard that taking a bath in tomato juice would help but his mother didn't want to use tomato juice for that purpose. On one occasion, his oldest brother told him that if you hold the skunk by the tail, it can't spray. He was wrong.

Paul got a face full of spray that stung his eyes. So much for attempting to catch a skunk and avoiding being sprayed.

Paul continued with another skunk story. Forty years later, Paul and his wife visited her father. He was in his mid-eighties and lived alone on his farm. He greeted them with a freshly skinned skunk skin which he asked Paul to take to Berman Buckskin to have it tanned. The skin didn't smell and neither did he.

Paul was curious, so he asked, "How do you catch a skunk without getting sprayed?"

His father-in-law answered, "You just choke it to death." (That sounded like Paul's brother telling him that 'a skunk can't squirt if you hold it by the tail'.) Obviously, that choking method required an explanation. Paul's father-in-law explained, "I took a long stick and tied a loop of twine to the end. Then I slipped the loop over the skunk's head and twisted the stick, choking it to death." He correctly explained that the skunk didn't know who the enemy was, so it never sprayed.

That, however, was not the end of the story. Paul had the fur tanned and returned it to his father-in-law hoping that someday he might inherit it. Unfortunately, just a few months later, his father-in-law's nephew visited him from California and asked for the skunk fur. The fur went to California where it resided for several decades. One day, Paul's wife got a call from the wife of her cousin in California. Her cousin had died.

His wife asked if there was anything she would like as a memento of her cousin. Paul's wife responded with no hesitation, "The skunk skin."

Her cousin's wife replied, "I'm sure there will be no other demand for that. I'll send it by return mail." Paul still has that skunk skin. He showed that skin to his grandchildren when he told them that story.

After lunch with the author, Meghan and Martin were ready for the plans they had made after the book signing, so they said goodbye to the author. They visited the science museum, and on the way, they tried to find all the Peanuts sculptures that were currently gracing the downtown area. Martin treated Meghan to dinner at an upscale restaurant surrounded by a large garden of beautiful flowers, a water wheel, and a small stream.

Meghan felt beautiful among it all. They both had roast duck, wine, and a chocolate dessert. It came easily to profess love to each other with a meal and setting like that.

They came back to the hotel and decided to stop for an after-dinner drink in the hotel bar. They enjoyed people-watching and just being together in a comfortable relationship. When they got to Meghan's door, she invited him inside. They hugged and sat down on the loveseat in the room. There was a feeling of love and desire in the air. They hugged and touched and kissed for a long time.

And then they were rolling together and moved toward the bed where they helped each other with clothing until there was enough off for sex. Meghan felt his body next to hers and his hand touching her between her legs. A huge heightening of tension and excitement swept over her. The feelings continued as his erect penis slipped inside her. Oh, it felt pleasant and exciting at the same time.

After many minutes of fervent pelvic activity, a drifting down of tension and excitement occurred as calm began to return to Meghan. She clung to Martin for several minutes. She looked at his face and realized that she had begun a new phase of their relationship. She hoped that she saw the same look on his face. Not much was said as they re-dressed. "I'll go back to my room," said Martin. "I'll see you at 8."

They clung to each other and kissed goodnight, and then Martin went to his room.

At breakfast, Meghan watched his face carefully as she said, "Last night was a night to remember." A warm feeling passed through her.

Martin agreed. "We must get together again," he said with a smile. After orienting their conversation toward going back to school, they drove back to their town and their separate abodes. Their communication picked up considerably after that trip out of town. Their contacts didn't necessarily have much content, just the sense of contact like, 'Hi, what's happening?', 'Everything OK?', 'Good to hear your voice'.

A few weeks went by mostly with work for Martin and Meghan along with an occasional snack in the hometown hangout. But one day, Martin called her to tell her, "I've been called into the dean's office."

"Why?"

"A student complaint. I'll call you after the appointment."

"I was called into a dean's office once," Meghan informed Martin.

"What for?" Martin asked.

Meghan answered, "I had just started teaching a communications class when I was a grad school assistant. When I got into the dean's office, I was invited to sit in the chair in front of his desk. He proceeded to tell me that he had gotten a letter from a Christian Social Research store, from which he then quoted. 'Your professor showed our literature, and she can do more damage in five minutes than I can fix in a lifetime of research. Make her stop'.

"What had I done? I had lectured on the topic of prejudice and had used an example of a printed sheet that I had seen at a party. The sheet had an orangutan at the top on one side and on the other side a photo that pictured a businessman. Under the orangutan were statements to the effect that blacks were descended from apes and under the businessman were statements that Jews owned everything. The dean went on to reassure me.

"He said that he had responded to the letter and informed the woman that 'We can't put that kind of pressure on our faculty'. I was relieved and appreciated his support. How did the letter writer find out that I had shown her sheet? Among my hundred and twenty-five students was a guy who worked at her store. So, you never know who's listening to your lecture. Well, at least he was listening! Missed the point, though."

Martin responded, "That's like an experience I had as an undergrad. I had written an article for the school's student newspaper. I pointed out that the United States was bragging about the hundreds of millions of dollars we were spending to help third world countries. That was the term used to describe what was left of the world after the First World-Western industrialized world and the Second World-the Communist World.

"In my letter, I pointed out that most of those millions were used to build infrastructure to help American-owned mining companies process and export their goods from the third world countries to the United States. Thus, American taxpayers were paying so that the American companies could increase their profits. In other words, American foreign policy money scarcely helped the economies of the poor countries.

"The assistant to a US senator wrote to the college dean complaining about the 'anti-American' content of the letter. I'm not sure what the senator's assistant suggested the college should do about it but the dean passed the letter on to the chair of my department. My department chair told me that he had responded to the senator's assistant, informing him that the school encouraged freedom of expression and in this case, the letter may have had some factual basis."

"These earlier experiences of ours ended well," Meghan tried to reassure Martin.

But Meghan was very concerned about Martin's current call from the dean since more and more professors were being challenged by students who expressed discomfort with what they heard in the classroom. The complaints were typically against legitimate classroom material, but that didn't necessarily matter to administrators afraid of controversy and donors. So, Meghan was anxious to hear the outcome of the visit to the dean's office from Martin.

Martin called to tell her that the student had complained about lecture comments and his answers to questions related to the class material in a class on sexuality and society. Martin had given statistics on LGBTQ people indicating that those who identified themselves as such were upward of ten percent and that the expectation was that in the next decade, the percentage would go higher. A student asked what these people actually do to express sexuality.

Martin answered, "Well, they use the parts they have as heterosexuals do, including hands, rubbing, body openings, and mouths."

The male student had objected and walked out of the class to the hall muttering, "That's sinful." The specific complaint stated that the student said he was uncomfortable with the discussion.

Martin had responded, "Sometimes some discomfort leads to learning something new."

Martin explained to the dean that since the material had been posted in the class description and on the syllabus for the class, the student had ample time to investigate what the topic included before the class. "Putting pressure on professors about legitimate subjects violated the principle of academic freedom," Martin said he had told the dean.

The dean told Martin that he was suspended from classes for a week during the investigation. He would be informed at that time as to how the situation would be handled.

Meghan suggested that they meet to discuss the issue at a local hotel bar where students would not be present. When they were seated, she reached across for his hand. Martin went over the whole episode with the dean. Meghan completely agreed with Martin's position. They discussed what had happened to others in such situations. In some cases, administrators had told complainers that the school couldn't put that kind of pressure on teachers, and in other cases, faculty had been terminated without a hearing.

Martin suggested that since he had time on his hands this week, he would like to make dinner for her. Meghan immediately agreed. Martin asked her, "What would you like? I like to grill, burgers, and fish?" They agreed on fish and made a date. Meghan was aware that research has said that many women do not plan for sex. This lack of planning frees them from feeling responsible for 'events'. But in a fleeting moment, Meghan did think about the clothes she would wear to their dinner.

When Meghan arrived, Martin had appetizers, wine, and music ready. They hugged and kissed and sat down to the refreshments Martin had prepared. They talked about anything but school—the weather, national politics, and even cars. Meghan wanted him to hold her and she wanted to put her arms around him, but she didn't make a move in that direction. Dinner was relaxed with light conversation about graduate school days and hometowns.

After they finished and lingered for a while, their eyes met with 'Yes'. They got up from their chairs and they rushed into each other's arms and worked their way to his bedroom.

In bed, Meghan helped remove their clothes. She was in Martin's arms and he asked her if she would like him to stimulate her orally before intercourse. Not sure what he meant, she agreed. Martin lay alongside her with his head near her vaginal parts. He gently separated her labia, put his mouth over her clitoris and began to massage it with his tongue. "Ohh," Meghan let out a happy sound.

Then she further responded with more excited and tense high-pitched squeals. When his tongue dipped to her vulva, she made a low-pitched reaction and when he went back to the clitoris, she resumed the high-pitched sounds. She felt her body parts swelling. This went on and on and she suddenly had a huge reaction with full body tension and then relaxation as her clitoris became tender.

She felt him on top of her and Meghan guided his penis through her labia and into her vagina. She found this both soothing and relaxing as they both moved up and down until they both reached a height and then relaxed. They lay there together in each other's arms for a long time in comfort and contentment. There were no words for a while and then, "That was wonderful," said Meghan.

Martin agreed, "We must do that again sometime." Meghan smiled and nodded.

After dressing, Martin made tea and they sat for a while, more quietly than usual. Martin told her, "I learned about oral simulation from a friend at Bible college who had gotten the information from a Marriage and Family course professor!”

“Wow! I didn't know that they would teach anything that practical at Bible college,” Meghan observed.

Finally, Meghan said, “I have to leave. My car shouldn't be seen outside your place in the morning.”

Beth had to put the book down. *I don't know what to think about their sex,* Beth thought to herself. “They certainly can keep sex from getting mechanical and even boring, I guess. I don't know what John would think if I suggested that. We haven't done much exploring like that.” She thought about how she was already pregnant when she got married, so they had to get right into family life instead of having much time for the two of them together before children.

She remembered how John, who always counted on 'pulling out', failed to do that in time once. He was too tired from the demands of school and the farm. “That's all it took, a few minutes, and our lives were set. Kind of like the couple in *Our Town*, I guess. But we were OK with that. This is what we intended for our lives, to be married and have a family, so I'm happy with my life even if it gets a bit much sometimes. But Meghan's life does sound exciting.”

Beth returned to the book several days later. “My life hit a period of 'a bit much' as my children caught pinkeye at preschool and needed drops. I did my best to pretend to give drops to a doll to distract them from their own, with only partial success. Then it was the deadline for the ads at the office besides the usual meals, clothes washing, and the rest of the regular routine." But now Beth had a few moments before she went to bed. She continued reading.

Martin became much more attentive. Meghan received some kind of contact from him nearly every day. The contacts cheered and warmed her. *The relationship required time but she could be more efficient*, she thought. He was worried about the outcome of the complaint at school. Finally, that was resolved by moving the student to a Spanish class for his language requirement. There should be less interaction with his own conflicts there.

Martin went back to classes but his enthusiasm for his work was tempered. His enthusiasm for Meghan and a longer-term relationship had been enhanced though.

At least once a week Meghan saw Martin. One night, they were sitting on her couch watching a movie. It was comforting for both to sit together quietly. When the movie ended, Martin was silent for a few minutes. Then turned to her and said, "I wonder what it would be like to be married."

Meghan answered, "I think it would be nice."

Martin responded, "I wouldn't be afraid of being with you always, but maybe not in this town."

"I wouldn't be afraid either," Meghan smiled at him. "I don't have to be here. I'm not even from here."

They decided that night that they loved each other with both repeating over and over, 'I love you'. So, they decided that they would get married at the end of the term, early in the summer. Of course, the engagement was not a well-kept secret on a college campus. One day in Meghan's class, she began the class with this. "I think that many of you have heard the rumor that I am getting married. I want to inform you that I have been involved in a study on rumor transmission on a college campus."

There was a collective gasp in the class. Then Meghan reassured them, "You heard correctly. I am getting married this summer." A sigh of relief from the class.

Meghan and Martin needed to make calls to their families to tell them about their marriage plans. They explained to both families that they had met at the university where they both teach. Both families were surprised, though reassured that the couple met because they had been working together all year. Martin's mother asked him if he was sure. "Yes," Martin answered.

He turned to explain his conversation with his mother to Meghan. Martin told Meghan that his mother had once told him that she hoped that he would find a girl near their farm but she didn't bring it up again on the phone though. She just said that she would look forward to meeting Meghan. "When can you bring her to the farm?" They made plans for a visit in a month.

Meghan's father answered the phone call from Martin. Martin told him of their plans and requested his blessing which her father gave him. Her dad asked to speak to Meghan. Her dad told her he was surprised as this was kind of sudden for him but he looked forward to meeting Martin. "I'll try to see it as gaining a son," he told Meghan.

Her family wanted to meet him, and Meghan promised, "That will happen soon."

Martin decided that he and Meghan should celebrate. His idea was that they should drive to the Twin Cities and spend a day of freedom from school demands. "I'd like to show you special places that my grandmother took me to when I was twelve years old."

Meghan happily agreed to that. She thought that it would not only be fun, but it would let her get to know him better. "Where do you want to go?" She asked Martin.

Martin had a list. "We can start at the art museum. Then we can go to Como Park and go out on the lake on the pedal boats. There's also a big merry-go-round that has beautifully decorated horses and benches with calliope music. There is a bust of Ibsen there too."

"Sounds wonderful. It all sounds like so much fun," Meghan responded excitedly. They decided to go the next weekend.

As they drove to the Twin Cities, Martin told her a story about the Ibsen bust. "It stands on a pedestal on a hill above the lake. A few years ago, it was stolen. There was no trail or suspects that anyone could connect to the crime. Years later, someone from Minnesota who was familiar with the theft spotted it in an antique store in California.

"The bust was brought back to its pedestal as quickly as possible. (It is hardly necessary to say, that the connection between the pedestal and the bust was strongly reenforced.) So, a happy ending, and we can walk right up to it."

"That's really an unbelievable story. I'm sure many people thought they'd never see it again," Meghan told him. "I look forward to seeing Ibsen."

They parked the car at the museum lot. Martin had his list of 'must see' items that he remembered from when as a boy. First, they walked to the 'Jade Mountain'. They each tried to count the trails up the mountain and find all the people carved on the sides of the large chunk of jade. "I think the people represent scholars," Martin told her.

Next, they went to the Atrium where a copy of Michelangelo's David stood. "Wow, that is impressive," Meghan said out loud.

Martin remarked, "It's a copy, but hey, this isn't Rome either. Michelangelo didn't sculpt it here. So, we can be happy with a copy. Now we'll go up to see the *Sea Nymph*."

And that is? Meghan thought. They climbed the stairs and there she was in front of them. 'She' was the subject in a painting of a beautiful mermaid with flowing red hair coming out of the sea holding a fish in each hand. "Beautiful mermaid and beautiful ocean colors," Meghan told Martin. "I can see why it impressed you as a boy. I suppose the lack of clothing impressed you too, right?" Meghan teased.

They held hands as they walked to another of Martin's favorite exhibits. Meghan felt so happy. The museum had been able to save a leaded glass window wall which now has a painting of a lake behind it to represent the original view. This wall was taken from a Frank Lloyd Wright home that had been razed. "It must have been a beautiful place to sit and gaze out at nature," Meghan remarked.

There were other Frank Lloyd Wright items there such as a sample chair. Meghan said, "I read that his chairs weren't all that comfortable. But the designs were artistic, comfort was secondary. It seems."

They continued walking through the museum toward the exit. Now Meghan excitedly pointed to the yellow glass chandelier at the entrance. "Look at that," she exclaimed. "Imagine blowing glass with all those curlicues."

They drove to the lake with the paddle boats. Martin paid for the tickets and they climbed into the boats. Both paddled and Martin steered. They both laughed louder than they ever had before when together they tried to navigate the lake. Meghan felt like a kid again, or maybe a teenager who didn't have to pretend to be 'cool'. Then they walked up the hill to see Ibsen.

"Wow, there he is, just looking over the park," Meghan described. They drove to the merry-go-round. "So beautiful," Meghan noted. Now they were both children again as they glanced at each other from their chosen horses.

"This day was wonderful," they said at the same time as they drove to a hotel. After dinner at the hotel, they fell into bed exhausted, immediately asleep in each other's arms. Waking up refreshed, they now had energy for love. The weekend had to end with breakfast and the drive back to their university town.

Along with class preparations and classes, Meghan and Martin made plans for a summer wedding on the ranch that had been home to Meghan. Martin's family lived on a farm near Climax and the two of them would travel from Minnesota to Nebraska. In the meantime, each planned to meet each other's family soon. Phone calls and pictures had already been exchanged.

One day when they were talking over coffee, Martin stated, "I just saw recent headlines which are disturbing. These statistics get reported and the world moves on. Women are being killed by their men. Rape kits are sitting unprocessed for years, so no charges. Probably one-tenth of rapes are charged, one-tenth of them brought to trial and only half of those get convictions. Not much justice in the justice system.

"And all that in a state that is supposed to be more civil, even nice. Now politicians are talking about getting warrants to inspect women's apps that track menstrual cycles! These reports are not uplifting for my class on society and sexuality."

Meghan noted his discomfort. "You did try to get at this in your panel report. The problem seems to be that too many people think that the way women are treated is naturally the way it is or must be. But it is people who developed these ideas and people can change them if there is a will. Just pointing out the problem makes people anxious when nothing is done about women's place in society.

"Too many sense that women are prey and are to be controlled. I remember my friends' conversation before I left grad school. There were many observations of our society from treatment of girls and women in books to the attitude of some boys in preschool to comments by men on the job."

Martin responded, "Maybe I should write an article or book where all of this is in one place. I'll start by pulling parts from my course together in one place. All in one place at the same time will make more of an impact. Politics is the place to begin dealing with all this, as women's bodies seem to get so much attention there."

Meghan was in thought. "That's a great idea." She remembered a photo she had seen of a high heel lying in the grass. She described it to Martin, "Women look at it and see danger, most likely a woman running away. Men may just see a shoe. Women were talking in my adult education class about the way they see the world.

"They must be watchful in a car ramp, careful in the dark, don't make eye contact, don't leave a car running, and so on. A man of about thirty-five said he had no idea that danger is often on women's minds."

Meghan went on to say that social sciences are not always helpful for the goal of women's equality. "I was talking to my colleague in the psychology department today." Meghan reported, "She said that a psychologist had published a study on morality. He concluded that women do not reach the highest, most abstract morality that men do. Imagine that!" She exploded. "The world is full of women caretakers, and they don't reach the highest morality? Have you ever heard of that?"

Martin answered, "Yes, I did hear that in a gender class I took in grad school. At the time, I was reminded of Ibsen's, *A Doll's House*, where the wife forges her father's signature for a loan (it would have to be a man's name to get a loan). She used the money to pay for her husband's stay in a warm place to recover from his illness. Her husband treated her with disdain for her illegal signature. There is your higher morality, sticking to a rule, regardless of consequence."

Meghan wasn't finished. "My friend also told me that a study on third graders' evaluations of each other after they had worked on projects concluded that the girls were not given the credit, even by themselves, for the work they had put into the projects. So, this devaluation of women starts young, even among themselves."

"That's interesting because I remember when I was in third grade coming home and telling my mother at bedtime about a girl at school," Martin replied. "I told her I couldn't understand why some boys at school did not like this girl. She does her work, she's smart, she behaves, but some boys took a popsicle stick and carved the end to a point and poked her with it. Her name was Ann. A clear attempt to establish dominance."

Meghan continued, "And then my friend was on the faculty at a school where they had invited an important psychologist to speak at their undergrad school. He inadvertently commented that women graduate students don't seem to be as creative as the men! Women can't afford to deviate much from being perfect in classes or they wouldn't even be accepted into graduate school.

"As if that is not enough, my mother told me that when she was in a college class discussing interest testing for different occupations, the professor said, 'Women do not have specific interests. Their main interest is in male association!'. Wow! Think of it, this reminds me of the undeveloped female characters in literature that I call cardboard cut-outs."

Martin resolved to continue developing these topics beyond the panel talks with the hope that more people would become more aware and begin a political movement going beyond 'Me Too'.

Spring break gave Meghan and Martin time to visit their families. Martin loved the ranch which sprawled endlessly. The big ranch house porch looked like the perfect place to have a wedding. Meghan also liked the cozy farm in northern Minnesota. Their families welcomed the prospective spouses as each family was afraid that neither of them would ever get married. Martin's dad said, "I'm surprised you could get away from all those books to even get together." Little did he know!

Yes, little did he know. Martin and Meghan left the books and got together whenever they could fit it in with their work. This kind of love was new to both and they managed to make the most of it. They also tried to fit in time to share other new experiences. One weekend, they traveled to a ski village and enjoyed the ambiance there.

They enjoyed the freer situation at the out-of-town hotel with an overnight where they could pay full attention only to each other without electronics and school papers. They had fun trying different positions while enjoying each other.

On the way home, Meghan said, "Well, we didn't break a leg while doing anything we did this weekend. You can tell that I didn't get a lot of time on hills in Nebraska! But I didn't need lessons for our other gymnastics anyway."

Martin answered, "No, and we didn't even see a helicopter take away a skier as I once saw. I loved the frost on the trees. It looked like a fairyland when we skied down the trail. And then the heat in bed was enjoyable too."

Meghan agreed. On the way home, they began to discuss their futures and how to bring them together. Meghan said that she had once heard a discussion on how to construct a life. "A person can choose where you want to live and get whatever job you can get there, or you can decide to go where you can make the best career moves."

Beth stopped reading to comment to herself, "John made the choice to live on the farm. He mentioned that most of his grad school friends chose to go to the jobs. I, however, chose John so I followed his choice. I wonder if Meghan will make the same choice." Beth resumed her reading.

"Yes, it's priorities. I would like to stay in college teaching and that means going where a job exists. Writing about women's place in our culture will help that. We haven't been offered contracts yet so we don't know whether we can even be here next year as an option. But we must be together somehow," Martin said with feeling.

"Absolutely," Meghan replied. "That's the priority. We can look around at what is happening in the faculty job notices. My specialties are somewhat more flexible than sociology, but we can both look."

Beth stopped reading again. "Well, I guess that answers my question. They will stay together. But what will happen if they get jobs in two different places?" She continued reading hoping to find the answer to that question.

Martin agreed. "I'll start this week. The journals have a section on jobs and the spring convention will have some attention to employment."

On returning home, school demands took up most of their time. Spring play practice had begun. Meghan noted that this play was a less controversial production than had been chosen for the previous fall term. "Of course, not everyone thought the fall play was controversial. What's wrong with a man being in charge of a woman, anyway, as in *The Taming of the Shrew*?"

But the spring production was a musical which required coordination with the music department. Meghan reported to Martin when they met after work for dinner downtown, "The music department is not in great shape to coordinate with anything. They have only a few members, and one of their main members just got terminated for involvement with a freshman student. When her parents found out about it, they were not impressed.

"They notified the president of the college who immediately terminated him without any formalities such as a hearing which is specified in the handbook."

Martin reacted, "Ooh, I always leave my office door open, full transparency. I just saw a new book by a woman seduced into an affair with a professor. Must be careful about giving sympathy, no touch, no deep eye contact. Can't depend on handbook protections even if a person is wrongfully accused."

"So now we have this musical, *Oklahoma*, scheduled," Meghan told Martin. "I looked at it and noticed for the first time how badly Jed is treated. I showed it to my psychologist friend and she agreed. So here this play was not supposed to be controversial but now we must put another disclaimer in the program. Good grief!"

"Have you noticed that we are constantly looking over our shoulders worrying about reactions and reputations, our own, or the school's?" Martin asked Meghan. "Last term, I had assigned one of two book titles. Students could choose. A mother called the dean and complained and said that I had assigned only one of the books. The one her offspring had chosen, *The Woman's Room,* was the book which was disapproved of by the mother. My explanation to the dean sufficed that time. But what next?

"You know, when we are looking at locations, let's keep in mind a larger school in a larger city. OK?" Martin asked.

"OK," Meghan responded. "You know, I've been thinking that I still want to teach and work with students. There is nothing so exciting as seeing a student seem to come alive when learning something new in class or chatting in my office about ideas or possibilities. Sometimes students who don't know what to do with themselves suddenly become alive when a new direction for their lives seems to hit them."

"I get the same feelings when I can see a student get insight into an idea that helps him or her suddenly see people or situations through a new lens. With that can come a big attitude shift which can be a big help in understanding connections and even a world view along with change in social or political directions. Not to speak of attitude toward self which often needs to go from negative to positive.

"For example, I remember the first time I told a class that masturbation was normal behavior. I saw a bodily sense of relief among young men in my class!" Martin remembered.

Meghan was also remembering individual students and their comments. Meghan said, "It's getting harder to get across the idea in writing that research references should not just be strung together as they get them off a computer, but that they should put the references into a new outline, synthesis in other words. I must help them take the concepts from articles and put them in new order with new headings.

"One of my sweet Native American students wrote me a note which said, 'Thank you for what you are doing for us. I understand what you are trying to do. After listening to others complain in class, I don't think they do'."

Martin said, "I also remember myself getting excited to see new ideas in psychology and sociology. Ideas I would never have thought of because I just accepted that the way things are done was just a given. One can't see clearly without somebody's analysis, often done by someone outside the main culture. Does a fish know water? You can't see by yourself."

Meghan continued discussing teaching style. "One must be careful to always realize that you are partially in charge of the development of students' lives. It's so important not to downgrade aspirations and to understand that development takes time. Break complexities into smaller parts. I remember when I brought my completed doctoral thesis to my advisor. He had asked for an outline. He said, 'I didn't think you could do this!'

"Why not? I had been in his classes and elected to Phi Beta Kappa (nearly all A's) as an undergraduate. I had nearly all A's in grad school. Would he have said that to a guy? Would any advisor have said that to a guy? Does one need a penis to write a thesis?"

"Maybe just a pen," mused Martin.

"Funny," Meghan answered.

"But," Meghan continued. "This was the department which added a new demanding course that students had to take before they could take doctoral exams. It was announced as the course that would 'separate the men from the boys'. I wasn't sure where I fit in, but since I had already completed the courses that sufficed to meet the current requirements, I quickly signed up for the doctoral exams and passed."

"In spite of everything, we would not leave teaching without some regrets, would we? We'll continue to look for work in colleges," Martin said. "I must get busy, tests to grade."

"Me too," Meghan said. "See you tomorrow evening."

Meghan contacted the music department about the spring musical. The professors there were cooperative but disheartened by recent campus events regarding their fellow faculty members who had been terminated and other staff who were being let go in some reorganization by the administration. Meghan met with the music professors and they offered to drum up alumni to help with their small orchestra.

They would have an orchestra for the first rehearsal date. "Whoo, that's some help," Meghan thanked them.

That evening, Martin and Meghan went over to Martin's apartment. A long hug at the door and they began their evening with togetherness. It was not as often as each would have liked as their work and the world intruded on their romantic desires. But Meghan thought that they made good use of the time they had. They got dressed and sat with a glass of wine and went over their days and projected ahead to their wedding and future job possibilities.

The wedding would be held at Meghan's family ranch. Invitation lists were being constructed by their families. Meghan and Martin started their lists.

Meghan started going over the day's highlights if you could call them that. The play plans were moving along but a snag had developed. One of the characters had some other ideas about costumes and stage positions. Meghan and the others listened. Meghan felt like just saying, "This is what we had decided and that's that." But she didn't and tried to find a way to use some of the ideas.

"For one thing, I don't like the corny rural tone of this musical. Can't we get something a little more modern in it or at least not so rural?" The student went on.

Another student spoke up, "What's wrong with corn and rural?"

The first speaker answered, "Nothing, there's just so much of it in this musical."

Meghan suggested, "Let's all think about it and come in with a response the next day." The next day, Meghan had come up with some small adjustments to costuming and set adjustments. Others didn't have much to say except to say that they had started doing it a certain way and they would get too far behind schedule if they changed much now.

But if we do that, the complaining student will be resentful and uncooperative at some level. Win the battle, lose the war, Meghan thought. "Students watch very closely, noticing how a teacher handles conflict."

Then another student complained about the 'bullying' of Jed. Meghan answered, "I've taken care of that in a disclaimer on the play program brochure. Maybe there's a way to temper some of that." At that point, they got back to practicing the musical script.

Martin said, "I informed a student that he had plagiarized his paper. I showed him where the paragraphs had come from an article on the computer. The student said he had not signed the honesty pledge and therefore, I couldn't lower his grade. Maybe he was absent the day I handed out pledge forms. Am I supposed to chase them down to get the signatures? Will we sue them for perjury or what? I failed the paper. We'll see what happens."

"Something new every day, it seems. Maybe it isn't every day, it just seems like it, doesn't it?" Meghan added. "I had a student who told me that his exchange student girlfriend was copying a paragraph from the computer straight to her paper. He told her, 'You can't do that'. Her answer was, 'That's what I have been doing and getting A's'. Head in his hands, he argued the point. We must be clear about this in our classes," Meghan declared.

"Yes, but I heard that an administration took faculty syllabi and put them online for courses to be taught by other people without any acknowledgment for the writer. They argued that they had paid the faculty for the work and therefore consequently they owned the syllabi. Really? We still have to tell students that the source of work must be acknowledged."

"Yes, I agree. Hard to fix everything tonight."

Chapter 6
Planning the Wedding

"What should we wear at the wedding?" Martin asked.

"Not cowboy outfits!" Meghan joked.

"Aaah! I was already imagining how I would look in a big cowboy hat!" Martin joked right back. Martin announced that he would like to make dinner for Meghan and another faculty couple next week, a psychologist G, and her artist husband, K. Martin said, "We need wedding rings and this artist designs jewelry. Would you like to look at designs and have them made? I could go over some designs with him and he could bring them along."

"I'd love that," Meghan said. "We were so busy with work when we first talked about getting married. I didn't need a diamond, so I didn't bring up the subject of rings. I thought we had plenty of time, but time is passing, I know."

Martin got a catered Chinese dinner for Chinese New Year and the celebration of the rings. While the meal was catered, Martin had gone all out with the setting. A beautiful table with a vase of small Chinese umbrellas and flowers in the middle greeted his guests. A Chinese teapot with small cups of tea stood on the side table. There was a bit of conversation about school events but mostly they all talked about wedding plans with occasional jokes about 'Home on the Range' for the music. Would there be buffalo and so on?

They all opened their fortune cookies. There were some authentic fortunes to make them happy with laughter such as 'You will have good fortune soon'. Also, there was some mumbling, 'If you work hard, you will have good fortune'. "This isn't a fortune!"

After dinner, they went to the living room to look at five wedding ring designs. Meghan said joyfully, "They are all beautiful." Some had stones and some were plain with inlaid patterns. "It will be hard to choose. Can we keep these and think about this for a while?"

"Of course, we have time," K responded.

After a discussion of various topics, Meghan said, "You know, the theater department is putting on the musical, *Oklahoma,* this spring. I would like to hear your thoughts on a problem I see with that musical."

"What is it?" Martin asked.

"Well, there is a song in the musical about a character named Jed," Meghan said. "Jed is a miserable, troublesome guy and bullied for it. The song describes his imagined funeral where everybody says wonderful things about him, essentially inviting him to commit suicide. The song is a comment on religion and society in that people say such nice things at funerals even though they don't mean it.

"But to encourage Jed to commit suicide so he could imagine people saying nice things about him? This is like the worst of social media long before social media."

Martin responded, "I never noticed that in the musical. I guess I listened to the tuneful music without much of a thought about social messages, but that sounds terrible. I'd say leave it out. Besides the cruelty expressed, the school and you might get criticism from the mental health organizations and deserve it. So, I say, leave the song out." K and G nodded in agreement. Meghan said, "We'll leave it out. I was going to put a disclaimer in the program but it's hard to disclaim something that extreme."

The guest couple gave Martin warm thanks as they said, "Good night." Meghan hung back for time alone with Martin. They headed for the bedroom, gratefully falling into each other's arms after a long evening with a few feet between them. Then nothing separated them for a time. Later, she helped him clean up the dinner remains and headed home.

All quiet on the school front for a few weeks. Musical practice was going along without incident. So were Martin's and Meghan's classes. Martin's sociology class concentrated on rural sociology which gave students an understanding of stresses in the countryside. It didn't necessarily account for the negative attitude of some rural folks toward city folks though. City people look at that dynamic and wonder about the basis for it, especially as tax money moves from urban to rural areas.

Martin said, "Students don't understand the animosity and frankly, neither do I, but it is a factor that needs some open discussion. There is obviously tension in the rural areas which shows in the suicide rate among farmers. Men who are farmers have a suicide rate several times that of other men. There are so many uncertainties with farming, from weather, to prices, to policies of government relative to farmers, that are sources of tensions and feelings of lack of control. Suicide is not a new issue.

"My grandfather told me a story about a neighbor years ago who decided to do away with himself by jumping into a cistern (a twelve-foot-deep water collecting cylindrical pipe dug into the ground). But the water came only up to his knees. It was cold. He stood down there all day, occasionally calling for help. Finally, in the evening, he heard someone come into his yard.

"A neighbor had stopped in to see him. The farmer in the cistern called and this time he got a response. His neighbor helped him get out of the cistern. My grandfather said the man never tried anything like that again."

Martin continued, "Suicide is not only a statistic for middle-aged farmers, but also for young people, urban and rural, in your age range. Statistics indicate that car accidents are the leading cause of death, followed by homicide or suicide, depending on the exact age bracket. These are all behavioral causes, not diseases as would have been true before modern vaccinations and antibiotics.

"Recently, I visited a high school senior in the hospital. He had been found hanging from a rope by his brother who found him just in time to save him. Later, I saw him playing his cello in his high school orchestra in a concert. How sad it would have been for him to be successful at suicide. He, like the farmer, has not attempted such an act again."

Martin continued his sociology lecture. "Now what is similar in these two stories?" He asked the students. "Various answers centered around this idea, 'they felt bad and that feeling went away, so moods can be temporary but death is permanent'." Martin went on to tell why the high school student felt so bad. His parents were selling the family home and buying a condo with only a couch for his bed.

Their reasoning was that their two sons would be in college and then they would no longer need the family home. Different folks have different kinds of attachments which are in their cores. We need to talk in families and tell each other what is important to us. We will go on now to other sociological statistics.

Meghan's classes were going along smoothly too, if one ignores the grumbling about required attendance and a written assignment on classes missed after three class absences. Meghan had decided students who are not present should not be evaluating faculty. Therefore, she wanted them to be present. Also, it avoids comments about a test such as, "We didn't have this," by a student who had been absent that day.

Suddenly, one day came the announcement from the dean and the president that the college was coming up short on the budget. So, there would be budget cuts, no money for supplies or student workers, or any other departmental expenses. The administrators would try to avoid even temporary cuts to faculty salaries. All grant budgets would be frozen as well. Martin was steamed.

"I saved some of my department budget for student workers so I could have help with multiple-choice tests at the end of the term. And now I don't even get my share as others have already used more than their allocation."

Meghan told him, "I'll help. I know you have that large sociology class since it satisfies a general education requirement, so you get more than your share of students.

Sometimes I sit in the back at faculty meetings and correct multiple-choice tests."

Martin heatedly continued, "Does the administration ever come up with a pleasant announcement?"

Meghan thought a while and responded, "Yes, if a big donation comes in, but that's not very often, and when enrollment increases. None of those are necessarily due to the work of the administration. More likely announcements have to do with more work and less money, so not positive. So, the reward perspective tends to be negative, all right. That is something they should pay attention to, the perspective that their actions present to the faculty."

Beth had come to a good stopping point in the story. Beth's thoughts drifted to a review of the various problems that college teachers seem to have to consider. "I always thought that it looked like an easy job, just talk a few hours a week. I guess they have to do more than that. Then there are the worries they have about keeping their jobs if someone disapproves of topics in their classes, or if someone in the community complains.

"The constant concern about the budget seems to make an insecure environment. After reading this book, I don't envy them, that's for sure. I'm glad I don't have people looking over my shoulder so much of the time like college teachers seem to have. There is my mother-in-law, but she seems generally happy with her son's wife. I'm grateful for that."

Beth picked up the book several days later. She glanced at the page. TJ again. "Oh, this should be getting more exciting now."

After months of no word from TJ, not that Meghan really expected any, came a message from TJ. *What happened to your documentary project? I never heard any more about it. I am finishing up my tenure at the university and planning my return to my family farm. I remember our time together this last summer with such fond memories. Someone whom I met in high school has also returned to my home area and reconnected with me.*

Before that goes any further, I wanted to check out if there is any possibility of our getting together for a future with me and a life on the farm. I could see that the house gets remodeled for us as my parents will move to another house on the farm. I could have linoleum installed everywhere, be easy to clean. I know I haven't kept up communication but I have been thinking about us. How could we ever forget our times together?

Whoa, Meghan thought. *Where have you been these many months?*

Meghan felt herself in conflict because she too could not really forget the wild strawberry field nor all the other passionate unions. "I think we are past the day when the woman is supposed to follow her man, no questions asked. The day is over when a woman is supposed to hold her development and future in suspension, where to live, what political party, what religious persuasion, until a man has chosen her that will then decide it all," she said to herself.

"Here I am! I'm engaged to be married this summer and up comes this not very romantic proposal." It reminded her of the musical, *State Fair*, where the suitor is trying to convince the woman to marry him by promising her that he will have linoleum put in the house, 'It'll be easy to clean'.

She tended to be busy for several days when Martin wanted to see her. Finally, she worded a response to TJ. *I was surprised to hear from you and surprised at your suggestions after so long. I thought we had both realized when we parted that we were going to different worlds. I have settled into my world here. I decided against being on a farm for myself when I raised a pig for the market. I had to pay my dad half for feed and when I calculated my income per hour, it amounted to about 5 cents.*

I prepared myself for a different lifestyle and continue to favor that different lifestyle for myself. So, I am repeating the same position that I left you with when we parted. We are going separate ways, though with much affection and happy memories. I have agreed to marry a professor at my current school. I wish you well. Best, Meghan.

Beth contemplated Meghan's TJ-Martin choice. "Meghan's romance with TJ certainly got my attention and reminded me of my husband's and my own early love experiences. But it seemed like a definite 'goodbye' when they parted. It is easier when one person in the couple at least doesn't have such definite plans for life. It seems it is usually the woman who doesn't have plans or gives up her own for her husband's plans, isn't it?"

Beth realized that Meghan had also made another decision. Meghan had chosen to leave the farm life of her youth and join the urban academic culture of the university. Meghan, Martin, and TJ had all been raised on a farm. Meghan and Martin had made a conscious decision to leave farm life and join the urban culture. Earlier in the book, Beth had been rooting for TJ and Meghan to get together and return to farm life but the two had already made incompatible decisions.

Only TJ would return to the farm. Admittedly, urban culture can be more exciting, but Beth thought to herself, "I too had a choice, I went to college, but I married John. With my decision to marry John, I automatically made more choices for myself. We returned to the farm. Life is not necessarily just one big choice but there can be many choices that can follow from one choice."

Beth went back to the book with anticipation. "How is Meghan going to feel about her choice?"

Although Meghan had been forceful enough in her message to TJ, she didn't feel as settled about the impending marriage to Martin. "Am I doing the right thing? Is it the best thing for me to marry Martin? The song, *Don't Fence Me In*, comes to mind from my Nebraska upbringing. Still, he doesn't seem to think he owns me. I am comfortable with myself with him. That's important. Is this what they call 'cold feet'? Unfortunately, I do remember the strawberry field well myself.

"Yes, Martin still has some vestiges of male culture left but he's not too defensive about it. After all, he does study relations between men and women and seems to apply his knowledge in real life. This all feels confusing. I'll get together with my departmental colleague friend. I need to talk to somebody about this."

Meghan called her friend, the one who had invited her over when she first came. They had visited from time to time and she felt comfortable talking to her. Meghan didn't want to tell her too much because sometimes if you do that, you don't feel so comfortable with that person anymore.

Besides, Meghan really didn't want it to get around that she was backing out on Martin. She did admit to feeling some anxiety though.

Her friend wasn't married so probably wouldn't understand. On the other hand, maybe that's why she wasn't married. They went on to talk about the current stresses on campus, including the anticipated musical that Meghan had to produce. Meghan's problem wasn't solved, but she felt better after the friendship shown by her colleague.

Martin called. "How's it going?" He asked. "When can I see you?"

Meghan realized that days had passed while she was occupied with her thoughts and work. They had not seen each other for a longer time than usual. "What about tonight?" She responded. She needed to clarify her feelings.

Martin arrived. She looked at him, and felt a funny feeling in her stomach; she guessed what people call butterflies. They hurried toward each other, holding each other in a long embrace. Their eyes said, 'Yes', and they headed for the bed. They seemed right to Meghan now. Being married seemed to be OK anyway. They spent the evening talking about the future. They informed each other about what future jobs they were considering. All seemed back on track.

The dates for the musical finally arrived, a performance on Friday and Saturday nights and a Sunday afternoon performance. Sunday's audience was filled with families with children and senior citizens who knew the songs. The audience participated in the encore song, and it was a joyous finale. Many in the audience greeted and shook hands with the cast. The community really comes together in performances like this.

Meghan was correct in anticipating a reaction to the treatment of Jed and so it was fortunate that the song had been removed. Still, there was ample evidence that Jed was a disturbed man and the community in the musical was not exactly a caring one. The local mental health organization left a pile of pamphlets giving advice on mental health services, at the entrance along with the programs for the musical.

Martin came on Sunday afternoon and he and Meghan went out to dinner afterwards. Martin praised Meghan and all the participants profusely. Meghan was relieved it was over and was more relaxed than she had been able to be for weeks.

Apparently, these were the days to get messages from Meghan's connections. Today, she got a letter (a real letter!) from her father. They spoke on the phone often but a letter. She opened it quickly worried that he had some bad news. No, it was concerns about her impending marriage.

My dear daughter, how is it all going for you? We know you have been busy with the spring musical. We are making plans for sprucing up the place for a summer wedding. Still on, right? I have been thinking about you. I have heard the saying that 'daughters are more important than wives to a man'. I don't know if that is true or not. I do know that men can take for granted what their wives do.

A man does know something about what some men are like and hopes his daughter never runs across any like them. Martin certainly made a good impression when he was here, but of course, we were not able to get to know him well in such a short time. Your mother and I heard a talk on marriage recently. The speaker spent time on the idea of expectations that couples have.

So much depends on what people expect and whether those expectations come true. When they don't come true, there is disappointment and worse. The speaker suggested that couples should talk about such topics as money, children, places to live, how they will divide tasks, and so on. I must admit that your mother and I didn't talk about those subjects either, but expectations were narrower then, especially when the couple came from similar backgrounds, but there are so many divorces now that it seems more important.

I thought I'd pass this on to you now as a loving father of his only girl. We look forward to your next visit. Your dad.

Meghan was nearly overcome with learning of her dad's concerns. She thought she would show the letter to Martin before answering his letter. So, she called Martin to see if it was OK to stop over that evening. He was happy to hear that she wanted to come, so of course, he agreed. When she got there, she seemed to be on a mission rather than looking for immediate intimacy. They sat down with a glass of wine in the living room where she pulled out the letter.

Martin read it with a sober expression and then looked up at her. He said, "Maybe we each have to think about this for a while." They agreed that they would get together next week and talk about those topics. Meghan reassured him that she didn't need to give answers to her dad but maybe just tell him that they would certainly discuss his concerns.

Meghan suggested they each write down their preferences and wishes on these topics so that neither would be influenced by trying to please to each other before even giving an opinion. She said she learned this idea in an organizational psychology course and it seemed like a good idea for them. They ended the evening with a kiss and an embrace.

Next week, Meghan and Martin came together to her apartment with their lists. After a warm welcome, they laid them out on the coffee table. Martin opened with, "Well, I thought we could have about twelve children like my parents have." Martin added when he saw Meghan's expression, "Just thought I'd start with some humor!"

"That's not exactly funny but I agree with the idea of keeping this discussion light," Meghan answered. "Actually, I have been involved with a group on balancing population with resources and their motto is 'One Planet, one child', so I guess I wouldn't go along with the idea of a dozen. I'm thinking more like one or two."

Martin had written down the same, so they went on to money. "Now, money is an important topic to me. I read that each should have a private definite allowance, no questions asked about the spending of it. That assumes, of course, that there is any money beyond the basics. Big expenses need to be decided together. We have to identify the basics and they come first, in other words, we need a budget. That's what I have, how about you?"

"I'm careful with money. I don't like to spend and I don't like to spend all my money, so I may have to be more generous with you than I am with myself. But if we agree on large purchases and decide how much is large, maybe we can come to an agreement," Meghan responded.

"Where to live, that is a question relating to employment. But maybe we can rule out some places and think about desirable places when we apply for jobs. I'm not open to everywhere," Martin said.

"Agreed," answered Meghan. "If possible, I'd like the same lifestyle as we have here except that we would be together more than we are right now. I'm assuming that we both have come from traditional marriages, with mom at home, and dad away at work. There might be an area for continual discussion even after we are married because I will want to do something different from that most of the time anyway.

"Maybe one day, we can discuss what we like to do or consider ourselves good at for the purpose of dividing up chores."

"This discussion is interrupting my passion. Come close and reassure me. You know, our relationship is new to me. I'm trying to adjust my whole self here. Let's have some wine and discuss sex. Better yet, let's do it rather than talk about it. OK?" Martin looked at Meghan.

"Yes." She got up and headed for the bedroom. It felt wonderful to lie down beside Martin and have him hold her. Soon there was some disrobing. She felt his face on her breasts. She felt him go down with his face between her legs, his mouth over her. It was strangely calming and exciting at the same time. Then she felt him going in with thrusts, both going into peak excitement, then relaxation with a few remaining movements up and down.

Then all was still, yet in an embrace. They lay back and Meghan felt filled with love. They ended the evening with Martin heading back home.

After a couple of weeks of welcome peace on campus came a crisis. Meghan got a phone call from one of her students. Her student is crying and said that she has been raped. What should she do? Meghan asked her what happened. "I went to a party of mostly athletes. There was some alcohol. I had a drink but others were drinking more. There was a lot of noise and this guy I was talking to said, 'Let's find a quieter place to talk'.

"I said, 'My room is right down the hall'. We went there. He locked the door and then I realized what he was going to do. I started yelling for help. People heard me but no one came. He pinned me down and I couldn't get loose, and he pulled off some of my clothes and pushed himself into me. After he finished, he opened the door and left."

Meghan asked what she should do. The student wanted it reported. So, Meghan called an administrator who said she would handle it and called the student. The administrator told the student that since she had let him into her room there was nothing to be done. There would be no case that would hold up in court.

Meghan thought of a saying she had heard. "Girls use sex to get love and boys use professions of love to get sex." One could say that maybe they both get what they want, but while sex is immediate, love is not necessarily forthcoming then or ever. Her mind went back to the free-for-all regarding relationships that took place before she and her friends left for their new positions.

Women often want to be held and cuddled. They don't necessarily consider it a prelude to intercourse, though that's often what they get whether they want it or not. Often it can be the end of a friendship, if not a claim of forced sex or rape. Communication on the whole topic is difficult as interpretations can differ between participants, depending on what they each wish to hear.

Meghan called Martin. She was upset. "This should have been reported to the police. Instead, the school gave no support to the student. I called the student and tried to do what I could. The police would have taken her to the hospital and a rape kit should have been given to her for evidence."

Martin responded, "Remember how many rape kits they are behind examining, hundreds."

"Yes, I do remember. But I will help the student complain to the administration anyway. There should be a policy to call the police, not just a policy that protects the institution from negative publicity. After all, the school is in the city, not a separate country, although one would think so sometimes. If I am still here next year, I will bring the need for this policy as an issue for a committee."

Martin thought to himself, "The chances of our being here next year are getting lower by the day. I need to concentrate on job openings now. The Sociology Convention is coming soon. They will have a list of openings. Also, the journals may list some openings. I'll contact my friends and acquaintances and tell them I'm looking. Meghan has to do the same. I'll talk to her about it."

Meghan had already begun networking with her graduate school group which had scattered when she left the university. She contacted the departments where she had studied about positions there and elsewhere.

Martin and Meghan met with their findings. So far there were no school openings that had listed jobs for both of their areas. If either of them found an opening, they would have to inquire about possibilities for the other at that school or nearby schools. They decided to look in the Twin Cities in Minnesota first. In Minneapolis and St. Paul, there were the most schools in one place in Minnesota.

They sat together and looked for openings there. They also looked for schools in other towns that had multiple schools. This was going to be a task for which they could only hope for contacts to help them.

An opening came up at the University of Minnesota for which Martin applied. A Fine Arts position opening appeared at another college in St. Paul. Meghan applied there. Both schools were willing to help them find a job for the other if one were hired. The processes were arduous. First, complicated applications. Then a written interview. Then phone interviews. If those were evaluated positively, one might get a personal interview.

One day in the spring, Martin got a call from the University of Minnesota for a personal interview. He and Meghan were ecstatic. It was a start.

Interview day came. Martin had to explain in detail what his specialties in sociology were. There were several different interviews, with individuals and with committees. Then he and Meghan waited for several weeks.

He was not offered the job. He did not have enough publications compared to other applicants. The heavy teaching load had prevented Martin from getting his work on gender relations into publication. They waited for news from their other applications. They would have to see what if anything would come through for Meghan and go from there. School was demanding in the last weeks of the term. They had papers to grade, finals to prepare, and not much time for each other.

In the meantime, Meghan and her mother were conferring about a wedding dress. Her mother liked to design dresses. Meghan asked, "Could you make a few designs, pretty but not too fancy for me to choose from? I can get someone here to make it." Meghan was glad to have a start on wedding plans as there were so many daily demands, she and Martin had been slow to get much done on details.

Martin called her on the phone. "Have you heard the news about the school where a student wrote home and said she was uncomfortable and her parents got state officials involved? It seems that her comment referred to her interpretation that there were too many Native American students there."

"Really," Meghan said forcefully. "I bet their ancestors felt the same way a hundred and seventy-five years ago! Here the colleges try to enroll more of them. I'm reminded of the psychology class where the professor reported on historical research on ethnic groups that showed that Euro (white) folks and Native Americans had the same average IQ. So, I guess that some people have felt that it was about time to remedy the disparity between them in education.

"Of course, whites never make a point of Asians testing higher on the average than whites. They often just put a quota on them for admission."

"Some of the Native Americans have complained that about being questioned with such questions as 'Who are you?', 'What are you?', 'Where are you from?', 'Where are you really from?'. All in spite of the fact that the person being questioned could speak in perfect English," Martin noted.

Meghan replied, "My psychologist friend and I were talking about exactly that one day, and she said that when people ask such questions, they are saying, 'You are in my white space'."

"It seems as if there are too many people coming up with problems that they have constructed themselves. What is a problem to one group is a success to another group. Glad the fuss isn't at our school this time," Martin said gratefully.

The flurry of spring activity had begun. First, the faculty must make plans for the next year. Decisions on theater presentations will be made. This time, Meghan was included in the planning. Someone on the committee suggested *Carousel* for the musical. Meghan had seen it but thought she had better look at it again before any final decision was made. She read the script and found something about wife beating connected to love! What!

She hadn't noticed that the first time she saw it. "No! Not again. We must get some shows with more sensitive values this time. No wonder people keep presenting *Our Town*," Meghan thought.

So, the choices were put off, although *Music Man* got some votes. The band could be included and that would increase participation. They decided to have a department open house before school ended with costume displays, historical playbills, and other memorabilia. They would invite the community and alumni. They would combine it with a fundraiser to supplement their budget.

The departments were also expected to plan courses for the next year. They were given a limited number of courses, so some would have to be offered every other year. The budget was never set until the next fall enrollment figures were sure, but plans had to be made on the predicted enrollment anyway. If there were a budget shortfall for the school, there would be some course cuts.

The cuts would be mostly for part-time faculty called adjuncts, but there could be some reassignment of some full-time faculty. Both Martin and Meghan had to participate in these decisions even though they had incomplete data.

Then, there were many social events to help celebrate this year's graduates. Spring dances, breakfasts, honorary organizations' inductions and dinners, convocations, announcements of graduate honors, graduate school awards, and graduation day practice to name some of these events. Martin and Meghan were asked to help with many of these events, so it got busier than usual.

They were popular with students and were receiving compliments from the students and parents. So, all in all, a busy but rewarding time as well.

Martin called Meghan. "We need to get our pick of the ring design to my artist friend. He called last night. Is it OK if I come over this evening to make the selection?"

"Perfect," Meghan replied. "We can have a relaxing evening watching a movie after we pick the design." They finally got the design selected that evening. It was a washer ring with two hearts overlapping etched on the front of the ring. Their evening ended as it often did, in bed with loving words and actions. Martin said, "I so look forward to being together until morning every day." Meghan agreed with that.

Now, there was pressure on the arts committee to make selections for the play and the musical for next year. They did pick *Music Man* for the musical, a quintessentially American idea of endless optimism with the 'think' method for learning a skill. Various suggestions were given, including *Lady Chatterley's Lover*, or *Boys and Girls*, about toxic violent masculinity.

Members laughed but all knew that the suggestions were sarcastic or an attempt at humor by someone who was tired of meetings. The play they agreed on was *Wizard of Oz*. It has a good size cast and would appeal to the whole family, good for the Sunday show.

Martin called to report a news story from a neighboring college. "My friend from a nearby college called to tell me about their latest crisis. A tenured professor teaching from a black writer's book quoted some words from that book. Students complained and he was suspended and then terminated or forced to resign. Without a hearing either. Problem is, he had just completed a history of the college which is supposed to go on sale at Homecoming in the fall!"

Meghan responded, "That should be embarrassing when the book signing takes place!"

"My friend's department as well as many others are quite dispirited over this," Martin replied. "It reminds me of a class on 'Marriage Counseling' I took in graduate school. The professor used as many slang words as possible for sex or body parts that many consider in poor taste at least if not just plain offensive. I think he did it to decondition us to those words in case clients used them in counseling sessions.

"Of course, we didn't have students complaining about teachers making them 'uncomfortable' with topics in classes at that time. It's difficult to predict reactions to our teaching these days. Our culture doesn't always recognize expertise if they don't like the information.

"And now we are being directed on what we can say or told to say nothing about slavery. Many people don't want any attention to this horrific part of our country's history. However, black history is a big part of American history whether people like it or not. Think about how many public and historical buildings they built that we still use," Martin added.

"Teaching is getting harder when we are expected to second guess what we say out of fear of losing our jobs," Meghan replied with stress in her voice. "I'll change the subject to a happier one. I took the dress design over to a woman who sews for customers. She will use patterns she has, measure me, and construct the wedding dress." Meghan visualized the dress to herself. "It will be white lace for the sleeves and across the top of the dress with a V at the neckline so my mother's white pearls will show."

The next time Meghan and Martin were together, she also told Martin, "I have checked into the ceremony language with the minister. We can add words to the official version. I told him that I did not want to have the word, 'obey' in the ceremony. That word seems to be in the standard American church versions.

"The minister said, 'That's no problem. We'll use the old service the early immigrants used. It doesn't have the word obey in the service'. Apparently, that was added after the immigrants became more Americanized," Meghan added. "Earlier immigrant women apparently had more power than they had later. They did have some power, however, as the Ladies Aid often held the money from their fund-raising dinners. Money talks."

Martin had listened patiently. Meghan asked, "Are you in with leaving out 'obey'?"

Martin finally got a chance to respond. "Sure, I didn't really think that your obedience to me was in the deal anyway. It doesn't sound like much equality for the woman if she must promise to obey. I never thought much about that though, now I realize it was in all the weddings I've attended. I suppose women, at least some women, are most likely to notice that word in weddings.

"It might be traditional, but not necessary at all. That's a reminder of the idea that women are property as we have discussed."

Meghan thought out loud, "It's kind of disgusting, really. But you know the Equal Rights Amendment hasn't passed yet either. That attitude sets a pattern that allows even educated men at work to consider that 'equal' women are lower and shouldn't challenge the men even by asking questions."

Beth stopped reading to think about her own wedding ceremony. "The word 'obey' must have been there but I hadn't paid much attention to the actual words. There are generally some words to the effect that the groom is supposed to treat his wife with love and respect, but I guess it still leaves him as the boss, doesn't it? The wedding was over so fast. Interesting that in a few minutes, a lifetime is supposed to be set in place.

"I wonder how all of this will be for my little girl. If she stays in the same kind of place as we have here, then she will know what to expect, but if she goes away like Meghan, what will it be like for my girl then?"

Beth continued reading.

Graduation day was fast approaching. All constituencies of the college were briefed on how to act that day, where to be when, what to do when, what to wear, and so on. In addition to marching in and out of the auditorium, listening to speakers, and a seemingly endless list of spoken graduate names, Martin and Meghan must greet the parents at parents' sessions, attend luncheons for retirees, and receptions. Parents and students thanked the faculty.

The faculty, including Martin and Meghan, received compliments, 'You changed my life'. Of course, the response was always, 'No, you did'. But the compliments were always good to hear anyway. Parents credited Martin and Meghan for helping their wayward children get direction and goals in their lives. So, graduation exercises and receptions were a happy time on campus.

For some faculty and staff, graduation brought back some upsetting flashbacks too. On graduation day, several years ago on a neighboring campus, their faculty received the news that the estranged husband of a graduating student requested a meeting with his wife in the parking lot of a convenience store. He shot her on her graduation day. She had been a student older than the traditional age.

She was stepping out of the role her soon-to-be ex-husband had wished for her. This reaction is not uncommon in cultures, including ours, where people try to hold back a person in their midst from achieving more than others. But for many people that was a terribly sad day.

With all the grading, graduation activities, and end of the year meetings nearly over, Martin and Meghan concentrated on the next year's employment matters. Neither had received contracts at their current school as that school was late with letting out contracts. But they had not received termination letters either. Department chairs were assuming that they would be rehired.

Martin had also applied to Twin City Schools. Meghan had been invited to continue the process at one of the schools to which she had applied, and she had just been offered a position there, but so far Martin had no similar offer. The administrators at the school where Meghan had been offered a position, offered to see what they could do for Martin.

They did come through with a position also for Martin. However, they still had no contracts from their current school, so their department chairs went to the school administrators to get a word of encouragement for their faculty members' continuation at the school. The administrators told the chairs that they had not finished the next year's budget and couldn't promise anything.

Meanwhile, Martin and Meghan were continuing with wedding plans. Before they traveled to Nebraska, there were dress fittings and they had to pick up their rings. Next, they planned to visit Martin's family in northern Minnesota. So, they made that visit while they were waiting for employment contracts for the following year.

There were several of Martin's siblings and his parents waiting for Martin and Meghan when they drove into his family farm. All were excited to meet again. Martin's mother welcomed them in and said, "Here, I'll take you to your rooms where you can put your luggage."

Meghan, Martin, and his mother joined the other family members who were waiting in the living room where they all participated in small talk, the weather and local news, while avoiding politics and religion. After lunch, Martin and Meghan discussed wedding plans with his family. Martin's younger sisters listened with rapt attention to every word. His younger brothers hung around at a distance with ambivalent facial expressions.

Meghan showed Martin's family pictures of her home. "Here's the porch and yard where we will have the wedding." They also showed pictures of their rings and Meghan described her dress and Martin's suit. Meghan described her parents' plans. "They will have a luncheon for the reception after the wedding with a big white yard tent with doors and windows. It's likely to be hot so the tent will have fans."

Martin's family described events and activities on their farm and surrounding community. His parents described how they were handling the business and their relationship to farm policies on planting and selling the harvested crops.

They told Martin the news of who had been born and who died while he was away. Then Martin and Meghan went for a walk around the farm. It was mostly a grain farm but they had a few animals.

"Oh," Meghan spied the goats, "You are soo cute." The goats approached Meghan for a pet and a scratch. One billy goat pushed the others out of the way so he could get all the attention but Meghan tried to be fair by treating each animal equally.

The couple walked along the gravel road near the farm while Martin pointed out and described nearby farms and families. "Look at all the wildflowers," Meghan exclaimed. They picked a bouquet to take back to the house. Then it was time for coffee and more food. Martin and Meghan explained a little about what they did for a living. It was a time for adjustment to the idea that his family read for pleasure or for the information they needed, and Martin and Meghan read as part of their work!

Martin and Meghan woke up on the farm to a beautiful morning each in their own bedrooms. Today, they planned to drive around the community and see where he had grown up, where he had gone to school and Sunday School, and played sports. They visited his siblings who lived in the nearby town. On the way back, they picked wild strawberries on the roadside. They also took time to explore a secluded log cabin that Martin's brother had built on some woodland he owned.

While walking into the cabin, Martin told of previous visits. "A few years ago, I decided to explore the pond not too far from the cabin. At the pond, I suddenly was confronted by a large bull moose. Fortunately, the moose turned and went on its way. On that visit, I also checked out the beautiful Showy Lady Slippers that grow around the swamp. The Showy Lady Slipper is the Minnesota state flower.

"Later in the fall, we would pick pails full of high bush cranberries for jelly." When they reached the cabin, they were compensated for having been assigned separate bedrooms while staying on the farm.

In the late afternoon, they came back to Martin's farm to prepare for the evening meal. They would stay overnight and travel back to their university town in the morning. They were hoping for information on the schools they had applied to, hoping they would have information offering choices for their future. When they returned, the contracts from their school were in their mailboxes.

Meghan's schedule was changed so she was assigned another English course instead of American film. Martin had received a letter from the school that had offered Meghan a position requesting that he enter the interview process. He responded immediately as the current school contract had a deadline for signing.

Meghan and Martin drove to the Twin Cities for Martin's interviews. He was offered a position as well from the same school from which Meghan had received an offer. They signed those contracts and returned the contracts unsigned to their current school. They would be living in the Twin Cities after their summer wedding. They looked forward to all that a larger community offered, all the arts events, and all the other people in their respective fields.

They rented an apartment and a trailer to move their possessions into the new apartment. Meghan and Martin were in high spirits as they loaded the trailer. "You don't need this, do you?" Martin asked.

Meghan glanced at him. "Yes, I do," unwilling to give up her little ceramic dog. "I don't suppose you need this," Meghan joked as she held up a book on sex statistics.

They drove their possessions to the new apartment but they didn't take time to arrange items, so they left a pile of boxes to deal with after their honeymoon. They set off to the ranch.

Chapter 7
The Wedding

Wedding plans were now a high priority. Martin and Meghan traveled to Meghan's country home to visit her family and make final plans for the wedding. Her parents were excited to see them again. Her mother went over the reception plans for the food. There will be a punch bowl with a server immediately after the wedding and a country lunch of ham, potato salad, mixed beans, buns, and various items like pickles and herring. Meghan saw a picture of the tent, good for hot or rainy weather.

Meghan and Martin went to visit the minister who said, "Here is the service I told you about earlier. No obey. It is an older service from the history of our church." Martin and Meghan looked it over. They selected some music. Meghan's friend from graduate school will sing a solo. They now had the wedding rings. Invitations had been sent out and replies were being counted.

They designed the program of events for the day. The wedding was really going to happen!

On the way back to her family ranch, Meghan's thoughts had gone back to that last gathering of her friends. She felt again those ambivalent feelings about relationships with men they had expressed that night. "In contrast, I feel so grateful that I don't have all those negative feelings for myself. I hope my friends who were so negative can have some of the happy experiences I have. I'm looking forward to seeing some of them at my wedding."

Martin was also deep in thought. "I'm so happy to marry Meghan, but weddings are more complicated than I could ever have imagined. I guess they are not just for Meghan and me, but for a whole lot of others who are excited for us. Try to keep calm. Meghan seems so calm. I must be too. This will be a performance. Meghan's more used to performances than I am."

When they got back to Meghan's home, a photographer had stopped by the ranch to plan for photos on the wedding day. He set up some equipment to get a sense of how to arrange camera settings. He also wanted to meet the participants, Meghan and Martin, as well as her parents. Meghan is her parents' only daughter, so this event is a big one for them.

Her mother told the photographer, "Everything needs to be as perfect as possible." Meghan's brother and one of Martin's sisters would be at the wedding too. There would also be two of Meghan's friends for bridesmaids and two of Martin's friends for groomsmen. The photographer made plans for spacing, lighting, and backgrounds for wedding photos. All hoped for good weather, though in July, they hoped they wouldn't have to expect rain.

Meghan and Martin continued discussing details of the wedding and post-wedding plans. Meghan's family had a small cottage on the property where they could stay the night after the wedding. Meghan said, "Let me show you the cottage." She got the key and they walked to the cottage and looked around.

"What a sweet guest cottage," Martin told Meghan, "I will be so excited to be here."

"So will I and I will be relieved too to start our life more together."

Martin looked at Meghan with teasing eyes, "Want to try it out?"

Meghan looked at him laughing at his idea. "I think we should wait until we are married."

The two made final plans for a short honeymoon before they traveled to their Twin Cities apartment. They considered several special tourist destinations that neither had visited before, that were within a few days' travel from the ranch. After the honeymoon, the plan was to stop back at the ranch for a day, load up wedding gifts, and then go on to their new home.

After going over the list, Martin said, "Let's write our top two choices on pieces of paper and compare what we have." They each did that and turned their papers over, and they each had the same place, the Grand Canyon. So, the Grand Canyon was chosen.

The wedding day dawned. Meghan and Martin were up early for their 11 am wedding. The day began with cool air which was good. Festivities would probably be over before it got too hot. The bride and groom weren't very hungry for a ranch style breakfast. They ate a little. Meghan announced, "We'll check the porch and setting details."

Chairs were in place and a keyboard was off to the side. The lunch tent was in place and tables were set for lunch. A neighbor woman was in charge of catering the lunch.

Meghan and Martin greeted family members, gave and got hugs and then withdrew to their respective bedrooms to get dressed for the wedding.

Martin's parents, his sister, the maid of honor, and other family members arrived from a nearby motel. Meghan's mom came up to help Meghan. The maid of honor helped dress and assist Meghan with her dress and tiara borrowed from a local gift store. "Oh, you look so lovely," Meghan's mom exclaimed with eyes shining with tears. Excitement was growing.

Guests began arriving. Meghan's parents were greeting them as they arrived. They were directed to sit on chairs out of the sun under a shade umbrella in front of the porch where the wedding ceremony would be held. A decorated portable toilet sat a distance away from the reception scene. The attendants, pianist, soloist, and minister arrived. Meghan and Martin were minutes away from being a married couple.

The mothers, Martin's father, and all grandparents were seated. Meghan, her father, and her attendants were lining up in the tent to be ready to walk up an aisle between the chairs when the music was to begin with a loud chord. Martin, Meghan's brother, and the groomsmen came out of the house to the porch followed by the minister, and took their positions, all turned and faced the audience. Meghan's dad turned to her and said, "I love you, girl."

She replied, "Love you too."

Loud Chord! Marching music from the keyboard. The audience stood.

Meghan's two bridesmaids and the maid of honor each came walking down the aisle to the porch and turned to face the audience. The music changed to louder bridal music and Meghan and her father marched to the porch. Her father gave Meghan a hug and turned to go to sit with her mother. The audience sat down. The minister began with a welcome and the order of the service.

"We are gathered for the marriage of Meghan Johnson and Martin Fitjar." He began with a prayer for the bride's and groom's health and happiness. He then proceeded to give advice. "Always treat each other with the loving feelings you have today. Remember those feelings. They will need to have patience with each other…Please, may God bless this marriage we are witnessing today."

The soloist sang, *Let us Love One Another*, to the accompaniment of the keyboardist.

Then came the vows and rings. "Do you, Meghan Johnson, promise to love and honor Martin Fajar as your husband? If so, say yes."

"Yes."

"Do you, Martin Fitjar, promise to love and honor Meghan Johnson as your wife? If so, say yes."

"Yes."

"You may now exchange rings." Martin and Meghan gazed into each other's faces as each slipped the ring on the other's fingers. "A kiss will seal this moment."

The wedding party turned to face the audience. The minister introduced 'Meghan and Martin Fitjar' to the audience. The music began and they all marched down to form a reception line for handshakes and hugs from members of the audience.

People milled around, some getting punch, others finding name cards on seats inside the tent and waiting for the lunch to begin. The scene reminded one of the Scandinavian song, *John Johnson's wedding*. 'There was Charlie Olson and Emil Olson, and Gustaf Olson…There was Charlie Anderson, and Emil Anderson…and Charlie Peterson was there too'. But there were some folks with other names such as White Bear and a Johnson family who were Native American.

The meal was family-style with a server who filled champagne glasses. The best man called for a toast. "Meghan, we are very happy for you and Martin. A great looking couple. Aren't they?" There was clapping and raising of glasses. Their friends occasionally called for toasts with glowing short speeches about Meghan and Martin. Food was passed around.

People had assigned seating, so the most patient relative was seated next to Uncle Don who was bound to press his political ideas on folks nearby. Another sympathetic guest was seated nearby Aunt Jane who would be asking the people next to her if they were saved. Aunt Martha would have responded with, "I wish there was something I needed to be saved from!"

So, she was seated some distance from Aunt Jane. Most of the other guests marveled at how nice the wedding was and how beautiful the bride was and how nice her new husband seemed. Of course, the weather and the challenges of ranching and farming were also favorite topics.

The wedding cakes were served at the tables. Each received small sections of the kransekake (ring cake; a whole one was on display) and a piece of traditional white cake with white frosting on all sides.

The photographer took photos before, during, and after the wedding. Wedding guests wanted photos for their own cameras, so that involved more posing. People started moving around, greeting others whom they had not yet greeted, and greeting the couple. Finally, all except close relatives had left the ranch. The wedding was over.

And a good time was had by all.

The bridal party retired to the bedrooms to change clothes. Now in more casual dress, they assembled with the parents, grandparents, and close relatives for coffee and rolls in the ranch kitchen and dining areas. All chimed in with their observations of the wedding and good wishes for Meghan and Martin. Finally, the just married couple managed to excuse themselves to go to the cottage.

They held hands and ran to the cottage. Meghan didn't think Martin should try to carry her over the threshold, so they stepped over together. Someone had set the table with a white tablecloth, flowers, wine, French bread, and chicken salad in the refrigerator for their later supper. There were even two of the little frosted wedding cakes and the bride and groom cake topper.

They hugged tightly. "Now we have been declared one, let's do it." Meghan looked at Martin eagerly. They headed for the bedroom, disrobed as fast as they could, and jumped into the bed and under the quilt. Embracing again, Meghan found herself underneath and Martin sliding inside her. They both moved in synchrony and Meghan felt a 'golden glow' in her abdomen, and suddenly, relaxation came for both of them. They stayed in an embrace and fell asleep for a short nap.

"Let's eat," Martin said as he awakened. They dressed. He opened the wine and he and Meghan set the food on the table. They gazed at each other and touched hands often throughout the meal. Not long after they had eaten, they went back to bed. This time, they fell into bed exhausted and went right to sleep. Waking in the morning, they immediately went back to cuddling and more. Meghan thought of the song, *Sugar in the Morning*...

They dressed and packed for their Grand Canyon honeymoon before going into the ranch house for breakfast. After hugs and goodbyes, they set out for the Grand Canyon Hotel. They took turns driving, touching each other's hands often as they drove. They listened to the Grand Canyon Suite all the way. Just as they approached their destination, the music came to the thunderstorm movement. The skies clouded up above them.

"Oh, no!" Martin said sternly. "What if we get rain when we get there?"

Meghan joked, "It will just be a shower. Besides, I think we know how to entertain ourselves in the hotel room."

Martin responded with a smile. "I'll be happy to be entertained. We won't let a little rain spoil our wonderful first days as a couple."

First, they drove to the South Rim for the sunset. Meghan threw her arms wide. "Isn't this wonderful? The colors are gorgeous." The colors were spectacular after the brief shower.

Meghan and Martin were enthralled as they gazed over the Grand Canyon. A great beginning for their lives together.

Chapter 8
Beth Has the Last Word

Beth had finished the book. But the book wasn't finished with her. *I won't be able to forget this book,* thought Beth. "Meghan has new experiences ahead of her, some exciting, I'm sure, but some probably not so enjoyable. Me, I know what tomorrow will bring." Beth had been thinking about a comment from her cousin.

"People choose between picking a place where they want to live, or going where a career takes them, often away from their home. People go away to school, and they don't come home.

"I went to school nearby and came back home. Did I choose that? Did Meghan choose to live far from home? Did we choose or did life choose us? I don't remember the precise time when I chose to be here. When was it?" Beth asked herself.

"What did that choice do for me? 'You stopped developing after you got married', my younger unmarried sister told me. Really? Let me tell her how difficult it was to adjust to the idea that I couldn't plan my day when my first baby came. Baby planned my schedule. My idea of my schedule had to be done in between the baby's schedule. If that doesn't count as development, I don't know what does. It certainly qualifies as adaptation to change," continued Beth.

"I'm not a finished person. This is just a part of my life. I will still have much to do and many more chances to develop as long as I live. Even if I did get married, I am still a separate person."